MURDER ON THE ROCKS

Visit us at www.boldstrokesbooks.com

By the Author

Femme Noir

Kiss of Noir

Murder on the Rocks

MURDER ON THE ROCKS

by
Clara Nipper

2016

ISBN 13: 978-1-62639-600-5

THIS TRADE PAPERBACK ORIGINAL IS PUBLISHED BY
BOLD STROKES BOOKS, INC.
P.O. BOX 249
VALLEY FALLS, NY 12185

FIRST EDITION: APRIL 2016

CREDITS
EDITOR: CINDY CRESAP
PRODUCTION DESIGN: SUSAN RAMUNDO
COVER DESIGN BY MELODY POND

Acknowledgments

Forever thanks to my friend Maggie Paxwell, who helped me immeasurably and is a gorgeous sack of diamonds.

To Cindy Cresap: the editor with the patience of a saint.

Dedication

K
VB

PROLOGUE

M urder is a seductive story that keeps me hypnotized and soothes my itchy feet. Macabre? Maybe. But I'd like to see you walk away from it. Money and murder—the world's most fascinating subjects. Forget love; I left all that behind. Love is for sunny, squishy people, and I'm dark. Straight black hair and black heart walking on the real side of life where love stabs, strangles, and shoots.

I'm a homicide detective. I get paid to put it all together. Let me tell you something about my job. The more violent the crime, the closer the relationship is between victim and murderer. Murder investigation is a two-piece puzzle. One piece is the crime scene and it forms half the picture; the other is the family, witnesses, and suspects. Ideally, the two halves come together and form a complete whole and your case is solved. If they don't, either I've made a mistake or someone is lying. And I don't make mistakes.

CHAPTER ONE

Well, whaddya think, Rogers?" Officer Hill chewed his toothpick. "Call came in from the landlord. Thought the vic was a mannequin." I looked at the bloody mess and multiple bullet holes in the body. I flipped open my grandfather's Zippo, lit it, and did a fancy finger pass, twirling it from one finger to the other, the live flame leaving me untouched. "Lead poisoning," I said.

"Yeah, good thing we have you here to tell us the obvious," Officer Smith said, fiddling with his watch.

"Suck my dick, Smith," I said and stepped outside for some fresh air. The bright December day and the brown of the lawn and trees was a relief after all that fatal red. I removed an American Spirit from my pouch, perched it on my lip, and lit it. I loved this job. My cell buzzed. "Rogers," I said.

"Jill? Jim. Whatcha got over there?"

The DA. Not an ADA or an intern, the motherfucking big daddy himself, Hallelujah Jim Harrison. "Just a routine homicide. We got it." I gripped my cigarette between my teeth and began to click my Zippo open and closed to keep me calm.

"Any suspects?"

I rolled my eyes. "The usual, Mormon school boys, Amish mothers, bunny rabbits."

Jim ignored my jabs. "Make sure to secure the scene. I want the dirt bag caught."

The DA got fuzzed up over every little thing in an election year. "Yes, sir!" I said. Jim mistook the malice for sincerity.

"Bless you, Jill. You're God's own hero and I'm always thanking Him that you're on our side."

"Yes, sir," I repeated dully. Click open. Click closed. Click open. Click closed. It was hypnotic and as addictive as the tobacco it fed me. I pulled smoke deep into the black canyons of my lungs. Once, I had seen Jim laying hands on new hires. At the recent Christmas party, he gave me a gold cross on a chain. I waited until I got home to drop it in the trash. Fuck God in the eyeball.

"Just make sure you're thorough. Don't leave a square inch unexamined. I don't want there to be any chance of this case getting kicked. Air tight, okay, Jill?"

"Absolutely." I chewed the sodden end of my cigarette. What was he on about? This appeared to be a garden-variety shooting. Jim's involvement was unnecessary. "Whatever you do, fly under Jim's radar. Don't let him get involved. Don't become a pet of his or you'll regret it," my ADA friend, Marny Marlowe, had advised me on my first day. Too late, I thought, returning my phone to my pocket.

"Are we interrupting your coffee break with this murder, Rogers?" Officer Smith said over my shoulder.

"Nope. Just finishing up." I grinned, tenderly tucking my lighter away, flicking my roach into the dead grass, and following Smith inside. I rolled on latex gloves.

"Well, it looks like a burg gone bad," he said. "There was a helluva struggle. This guy didn't want to let his shit go."

I bent over the body and looked at his hands. "His fingernails are broken."

"And that's not all. Look at this." Smith guided me through the house. There was blood spatter on every wall. Back in the living room, I looked at the ceiling. "Up there too." I pointed.

"Jesus," Smith said. "What the hell is worth that kind of fight?"

"Your life?" I said. "This was overkill."

"Probably just made the assailant mad and he couldn't stop," Hill said.

"Wait a minute." I frowned. The victim was white, in his thirties, rough. He had six bullet holes and blood smeared all over him, but there was no blood from the wounds themselves. They were dry and clean. "Post mortem," I said. I turned the victim's head, and there was a red line on his neck. I removed a magnifying glass from my pocket, pulled up the victim's eyelid, and shone my flashlight into his eye. Petechial hemorrhages. "Cause of death wasn't shooting. This man was strangled. They shot him after he was dead and mopped him in this blood." I stood straight. "Shit! Whose blood is this?"

Chapter Two

It was a stormy December night when I got the call. Sheriff Perryman had a case just outside the city limits that she wanted my department to evaluate.

Having been newly elected and a female, the first woman sheriff in tri-state history, Dana Perryman wanted no mistakes in her administration. She intended to single-handedly transform the country bumpkin image of the sheriff's office. She wanted no more parallels drawn between Mayberry and the Tulsa County Sheriff. She wanted the comparisons to the Three Stooges to end. She wanted no more inmates lost in jail or accidentally released. She wanted no more deputies unable to understand a written court order. She wanted no more deputies napping in court.

In short, she wanted to eliminate the ignorant hicks from her staff. And that made her universally despised. She had been sworn in after the favorite white GOB sheriff resigned under disgrace and scandals of nepotism, racism, and cronyism. The rumor ripples and vitriol had been felt far enough to make it to me—the last grape on the vine. And Perryman wanted to repair the petty jurisdictional wars between city and county, so in the interest of cross-departmental diplomacy, I was called to go to the death scene and to take my olive branch. I was curious to get a look at this broad and very interested in how she got the job in a county that still wasn't sure about evolution or the solar system.

After I hung up from being summoned, I cursed the cold rain, put my box of dinner back in the freezer, got into my '86 Buick Grand National Turbo, and drove out to the freeway west of town. The rain beat like drumsticks on the roof. I blew past vehicles that had pulled into the emergency lane and under bridges to wait out the storm. I cupped my hands to my mouth and blew on them. My breath plumed between my fingers like steam. Predictions stated this winter rain would turn to ice any minute. I promised myself a hot bucket of chicken after I wrapped this up.

"Damn, where is the heat?" I played with the knobs. The low-down heater had never worked right.

The scene on the highway was lurid in the rainy blackness: smeary red police lights, headlights, spotlights, cars crawling by the detour, uniforms directing traffic with flashlights. The sound of rain on my car roof abruptly changed to the sound of sand, and I knew the ice was here. I skidded close to the scene, and a few officers jumped like gazelles out of the way. I pushed my hood into the police tape. I revved the engine a couple of times and turned it off.

The ice pellets dropped down my collar and on my hair and clicked on the ground like tiny glass beads. I stomped my boots a few times to warm my feet. The air was silent except for the encompassing sound of millions of ice grains ticking on the pavement. I walked through the barriers to a bevy of brown.

"Sheriff Perryman?" I said in general. Ordinarily, I didn't stop to greet anyone at a crime scene, but I knew tonight was different. The deputies scowled at me and parted to reveal the sheriff. Reading from top to bottom: white girl, of course, with thin brown hair clipped in a pony, no makeup, thick overcoat, and long legs clad in pressed brown uniform slacks. "I'm Detective Rogers from Homicide. Grrl, congrats on being the big dog!" I held out my hand. Wordlessly, she bit her glove to remove it and clasped mine in her own bony, chilled hand. "Spin so I can see whatcha got!" I raised her hand and tried to twirl her. The sheriff jerked her hand from mine.

"Detective Rogers, that will be quite enough," Perryman said, her voice colder than the air. "The accident is over here." She strode away and I stared at her trunk.

"Not flat enough for midtown but too flat for the west side. You sure didn't use that to win, so you must have got the goods on somebody."

The sheriff whirled indignantly, losing her footing momentarily in the ice pellets. I reached to steady her, and she swatted my hands away. "I was warned against you, and I am disappointed to find you are worse than I anticipated. I had hoped we would have a common understanding as two females trying to be successful in a male-dominated profession, but you have ruined that hope with your puerile humor. This is all going in my report."

"Woof!" I said, grinning. "Feisty! What say we stop flirting and get a look at this body?"

"Oh, for God's sake. You're just like these teenage boys calling themselves deputies," she said, kneeling with me over the victim.

Time to focus. I put a cigarette in my mouth and lit it with my Zippo.

"There's no smoking here, Detective," Perryman said.

"Where?" I looked around, a speck of ice hitting my eyebrow. I rubbed it away. "The earth? Let's get to work."

The dead woman was sprawled on the asphalt, her body twisted into a swastika, a scarf covering her face, a blanket of ice beads already pooling in her clothes and hair. I removed a pair of latex gloves from my pocket and put them on, an act that never failed to give my crotch a charge.

"The call came in about an hour ago from a passing motorist." Perryman consulted her notepad. "The caller said the vehicle never slowed down. The caller thought it was a mannequin. My men say it's just an accidental hit-and-run. Vehicular manslaughter."

I squinted up through the smoke and ice at Perryman. "But you had a hunch, didn't you?"

A faint smile twitched one corner of her mouth. "Yes."

I stood up, enjoying every feline inch of my frame. "And you called me," I said.

Perryman dropped her eyes. "Yes."

I crunched around the body. "How much tromping through this scene have the hillbillies done?" I smoked, enjoying the flare of coal in the middle of the ice storm. I exhaled a big blue cloud.

"None. The responding deputy secured the scene and called me."

"None?" I gestured to big, ice-filled boot prints pressed in the mud next to the asphalt.

Perryman shrugged. "Not ours."

"Then make sure to get that Cinderella evidence." I scratched my chin. "Have the rednecks been trained how to collect footprints?"

"Of course," Perryman said. "But let's do this together." She strode to her vehicle, got a can of hairspray for the fixative, the frames to press around the shoe prints, and the plaster of Paris to preserve the impressions.

"You've *got* to be kidding," I said.

"No, I'm not. Are you allergic to hard work and getting your hands dirty? Or are you one of those 'not my job' snobs? Get your ass down here." Perryman knelt by the first print. "Help me clear away the ice."

"Hey, I've paid my dues," I said.

Perryman gazed up at me.

"I've done years of getting coffee and knock and talks. You can pound sand," I said.

Perryman just stared at me. I sighed and crouched next to her. We worked together in silence until we had molds of all three big boot prints.

"So was it accidental?" Perryman asked.

"It's not a felony swerve, that's for sure," I said under my breath. I held out my hand, and without a word, Perryman put her flashlight into my grip.

Perryman's eyes lit up. "I knew it! What do you see?"

"Well, between the report and the deputy arriving, somebody came back and wiped the blood from her face." I barely lifted the scarf and pointed to the cleaned smears around her chin and throat that were only visible under the strong beam of Perryman's flashlight. "And he or she laid the scarf over her head. See?" I pointed uphill. "The direction she was dragged would make it impossible for her scarf to be over her head. And one shoe is on and the other one is placed neatly upright near the body. That loose shoe should be somewhere between her car and here, not sitting pretty right next to her. What a mess." I shook my head and motioned for photography to start recording the scene.

"So wait." Perryman held her hands out. "What is this? Accident? Hit-and-run?"

"Hell no. It's murder, Sheriff."

"You're sure?"

"Aren't you?" I grinned. "This woman was set up, run over, and dragged till dead. And considering that she was most likely killed on impact, that she was dragged so far after the collision is vindictive."

Perryman clapped her gloved hands together. "Murder! Thank you, Rogers."

A chubby, balding deputy with glasses repaired with duct tape approached. "Chief, you ready to send these boys home to their families? Ain't nothin' goin' on here, just a sad accident in an ice storm."

"Detective Rogers and I believe it to be murder, Gerritts. So no one will be going home."

Deputy Gerritts laughed. "Now why would you think that? I been a deputy forty-five years, and I'm sayin' this little gal had car trouble, got out to flag down help, and got hit. Case closed. Murder. That dog just won't hunt."

"Analysis of the scene indicates—" Perryman began.

Gerritts cut her off. "Now listen, young queen, we've a been takin' care a this county long before you was born and we done all right. Remember who you work for and don't get tangled up in the city's fancy theories." Gerritts spat tobacco at my feet. "Sheriff, you got to dance with who brung ya. This ain't no murder." He ambled away.

Perryman was red-faced. I regretted what a heel I had been and I saw the obstacles this woman faced every hour.

"Hey, Sheriff, I am sorry—" I began.

"Forget it," she said. "I don't need your motherfucking pity. I heard you were good at your job. Too bad you're just a throbbing hormone." She jogged away to give instructions to her deputies.

I smiled and flicked my butt into the darkness. Chicken time.

CHAPTER THREE

I started awake with a gasp in the darkness. I was shivering even though I was buried under the covers. The house was cold. I glanced at my bedside clock. Black. I reached to turn on the lamp. The switch dry-clicked with no light. Power outage. I stumbled into last night's jeans and boots and crept cautiously to the front door. The entire block was dark. I stepped outside onto the porch and had to grab my porch pillar to keep from bustin' my bone.

The entire neighborhood was encased in ice, and it was still coming down like sand sifted from the clouds. I inhaled, and the chilled air frosted my lungs. I cautiously wobbled to the majestic river birch in my side yard. It was sheathed in ice from top to bottom. Along the street, the tree limbs were dangerously bowed and reaching for the ground. The azaleas were divided and crushed by the weight of the ice. The hollies were split and lying flattened on the lawn; the arborvitaes were smashed to the earth as if they had been bulldozed. Everyone's landscaping was curled and sculpted into painfully unnatural shapes that seemed about to snap and break any second.

The quiet was so complete; it was like being vacuum sealed inside a drum. I slowly crunched out to the street, and I saw a neighbor in a coat and bathrobe, just as shocked and bewildered as I. "Trees are coming down all over!" he shouted, gesturing. "A million and a half people without power!"

"Shit!" I yelled back. Our voices violated the sanctuary silence. "Shit!" I repeated and sprinted awkwardly for the house. Once inside, I kept flicking switches without thinking and felt more foolish each time the room remained dark. I went to the refrigerator for a Pepsi and slammed the door shut when the light didn't come on there either.

When I banged my shin into the coffee table as I searched for candles, I had had enough.

I crept slowly through the house until I found my phone. I used the bright screen and my old cigarette lighter for illumination as I gathered clothing and prepared for a shower.

"If the water doesn't warm up, I'll stay funky," I said. Outside, I heard more big cracks followed by enormous crashes. I heard the ice still tapping on the bathroom window like impatient fingernails. The water did heat, and I took a fast rinse and dressed, needing to leave quickly because I felt smothered and suffocated all alone in the cold, dark, silent house. Before I left, I filled the tub and all the sinks with water. The pumping stations would eventually be stranded powerless too, I decided.

I stumbled to my car, wishing for crampons and an army tank. The car started, vibrating like a tuning fork. I backed all the way into the street before I realized I couldn't see a goddamn thing. I tried to pull back in the driveway, but my wheels spun. I was already stuck. I left the car idling and stood very carefully and edged my way around the car, chiseling ice from the windows. Ice pellets fell into my collar and slid down my back, causing me to yelp continuously, feeling more and more stupid. But I couldn't stop myself.

I got back in the car, brushed off my bristly brush cut, and tucked my fists into my armpits. "Damn, this storm has turned me into a shrieking goober."

I backed out, my wheels spinning a little, and then I sped down the block. I hit the limb lying across the road before I saw it. "Jesus Christ!" I yelled. I exploded out of the car and promptly fell on my ass. I lay there, fuming, utterly defeated when I heard laughter echo through the air. Ice pecked my face. I sat up fast, slamming my head against my open car door.

"Whoa!" I heard the voice exclaim. "Just sit still before you do any more damage."

I held my head. It felt wet. I looked at my hand. Bloody. A man in wellies jogged effortlessly down his steps, across the yard, and to me, where he crouched.

"You okay?" he asked.

"I'd be better if this goddamn ice would melt."

"I hear that. C'mon, I'll help you up and get your car free."

"Hey, thanks, man." We clasped hands and I stood.

"Nice car," he said, stroking the fender. "What is this, a Grand National?"

"Yeah, you got an eye, man. V6, turbo, four speed," I said, grabbing a hand full of ice from the roof, holding it to my head, and leaning against the body for support.

"Should you be driving a prize like this out in the weather? She needs to be nestled in a velvet box in a climate-controlled garage."

I rolled my eyes. "It's not pussy. It's just a car."

The guy shrugged. He walked to the front of the car and peered beneath. "Not bad. You're just hooked on a small branch. Start backing the car."

I threw the bloody ice into the gutter and sat in the car again. I put it in reverse, and after some bouncing, tire spinning, and yelling, I was free.

"Thanks again, bro. I owe you one!" I shouted as I sped in reverse down the entire length of the street to the first intersection. I crunched over a pile of limbs and headed toward the hardware store. Whether businesses had power was hit or miss. Most were closed and dark. The hardware store was open and bright. The parking lot was so full. I had to park half on the sidewalk and half in the fire lane. Inside, the lines were long and the shelves were picked clean. I looked for batteries—gone, car cell phone chargers—sold out, ice scrapers—gone, bags of sand—gone, candles—none, flashlights—

sold out, generators—all lined up in cashiers' queues getting bought by customers who were not clumsy, tardy oafs.

"Ya'll got anything left?" I asked a clerk who was restocking the gas cans.

"Hardly. We've got ice melt." He pointed.

I grabbed an ice chest and a bag of ice melt, and stood in line enviously eyeing the econo-packs of batteries that everyone else had.

"When will you get more batteries?" asked a man holding a baby in one arm and a toddler with his other hand.

"Supposed to be later today," the manager said, pressed into service as a cashier.

The lines were slow and the wait was tedious. I was behind a woman with an expensive haircut who was buying a basket load of batteries. When her purchase was finally totaled, she put her purse on the counter and began digging for her money. After some time, she located her checkbook, extracted it, and flopped it open. She gestured to the cashier for a pen. He patted himself down and shook his head.

I groaned. "Are you kidding me?"

She turned to me. "Do you have a pen?"

"Hell no, I don't have a pen. You need to get your shit together before you come out in public."

"Pardon me?" Her voice was soft and cultured.

"You are a piece of work, sweetheart."

"*Excuse* me?" She glared at me, her voice hard.

"Yeah, I'll say it. Who do you think you are, bringin' all that mess to the register and not even being ready? Can you pull your head out and realize there are other people in the world besides your privileged cracker ass and we've been waitin' a long time and here you are with your sorry *check* and no pen and all the batteries that God ever made. What is wrong with you?"

"How *dare* you! I have just as much right—"

"Shut it, softie."

"I demand to speak to the manager! I'll call the police!"

"Good luck, lady. I *am* the police." I said, the wound in my head beginning to pound. The cashier wordlessly gestured to the manager who was busily ringing up customers. The woman stormed off.

"Now you're talkin'!" I placed her basket of batteries firmly in front of the cashier. "I'll take these."

"Hey, can I have some of those?" the man with kids, standing in line with a bag of cat litter, asked.

"Sure, what size?" I parceled out most of the batteries to people in line behind me. I kept two packs for myself. The cashier rung up my sale.

"Do you have a pen?"

CHAPTER FOUR

I drove to Maple Ridge, wanting any diversion to keep me from returning to my empty house. I had avoided seeing Sophie Walsh. She had nearly captured me when I was in Tulsa before, and I had not been in touch with her since I returned to my hometown from a temporary madness in Missoula, South Dakota, and took a job with the homicide division of the Tulsa Police almost a year ago. She didn't know I was here. Well, today was her lucky day. This weather made the time ripe for surprises.

My mind wandered to my memories of Sophie in anticipation of what I would be enjoying later.

The geometry of that woman hooked me right where I lived. Sophie was steep slope and gentle grade, the concentric circles emanating from her hypnotizing me like a Bartok symphony.

But listen, I'm no brainiac loser; I only know who Bartok is because I followed a twist into a classical music elective in college and I learned about the composer before I could drop the course and quit the girl.

I was going to run my tongue from Sophie's ankle to the delicious crevices and interior angles and lose myself in her vanishing point. I was jumpy with eagerness. I panted and my eyes darted frantically. I sweated just keeping my car on the road and making the right turns. The arc of our overlapping triangles would bring me peace. The symmetry of our joining would settle and feed me. At last, I eased my car into the space behind Sophie's. I fondled the Zippo in my pocket.

I walked cautiously to the front door. Sophie had scattered salt and sand on the walk, which was effective until the new ice covered it. I stroked the front door as if it were cashmere. The algorithm would be this: me: "I'm here." Sophie: "Fuck me and never stop."

Grinning big, salvation at my fingertips, I rang the bell. Hearing nothing, I realized the doorbell wouldn't work in a blackout. I knocked and heard quick, light footsteps. I smoothed melting ice crystals off my flattop, smelled my breath, and stood up straight.

The door flew open and a wad of cash was thrust at me. I got a breathtaking view of Sophie's back. Her long blond hair was in a thick braid; she wore a white cable knit turtleneck, and her juicy rump was sealed into jeans tapering to boots. Behind her, I saw a gothic horror movie number of candles perched on every surface creating the perfect, soft, romantic ambience.

"Pizza's here!" she called into the house, her arm still extended to me. I leaned against the doorjamb, my eyes smoking her like a grit. Sophie finally turned to me with impatience and took a startled step back, her bow of a mouth falling open.

"Hi," I murmured. Now she could proceed to adore me. I licked my lips.

"Drop dead," Sophie said, the blue look of contempt not melting into sex and worship.

I took her response as merely an opening flirt. "I'm single and cold and I don't want to be," I told her, my voice low and hoarse. I reached for her, and she grabbed my hand in an awkward greeting and laughed uncomfortably. "So you do remember me."

"Jill." A noise behind her startled Sophie out of her scorn and into politeness. She looked over her shoulder. "Where are my manners? Come in." She giggled unpleasantly. "We found one pizza place in Broken Arrow who has power, and we bribed them to deliver all the way over here, so we've been waiting."

"Aw, baby, you know me better than that." I pulled Sophie into a blissful embrace. "Remember the meteor showers?" I whispered into her heavy, silken golden hair.

Again, Sophie pushed me away, and this time, she blushed and her laugh was like a bark. "I have no idea what you're talking about."

Suddenly, footsteps sounded down the hallway. A white man, toweling his chestnut hair, emerged dressed in cords and a sweater. "Well, at least we still have hot water. Sugarfoot, where's the takeaway?" His British accent made me despise him on sight. I touched my handcuffs.

"Um." Sophie made a limp gesture toward me.

"No pizza, motherfucker," I said, hating him and trying to glare an answer out of Sophie who wouldn't look at me.

"Ah." The man lifted his eyebrows and looked from one to the other of us. Sophie was studying the tip of her boot. "*No* pizza."

"Nope," I said then thundered at Sophie. "Who the fuck is this?"

Sophie clenched her jaw and rolled her eyes.

"I'm Alistair Bellingham," the man answered jovially and then asked with a smile, "Who the fuck are you?"

"I'm—" There was a loud pounding on the door.

Sophie sprang to life as if electrified. "Pizza's here!"

CHAPTER FIVE

My CV is this: I was an orphan, raised by fools who are now dead due to their foolishness. The only legacy I have is a number on the Native roles (which I have inked in the small of my back) and my beloved Zippo lighter I snagged from my grandfather's coffin before it was closed and sealed. It's a silver souvenir from his military service with "Rogers" and our tribe's insignia inscribed on one side and "Korea 1954–1956" and the quote, "I am sure to go to heaven because I've served my time in hell" inscribed on the other. My grandfather was the only man I've ever admired until Chief St. John. So although I was only ten when Edudu died and I didn't yet smoke, I knew I would need that lighter. I devoted my life to honor Edudu's memory so I studied hard, playing with that lighter constantly like a talisman. I earned a scholarship in theology from ORU. That's Oral Roberts Uni to those outside Tulsa. If you've never seen it, look it up. It's an architectural freak show and has been turning out closeted Christian gays by the thousands since 1963. It was originally built over acres of farmland and field, and though at the time, it was self-isolated because the street address preferred by its nutbag founder, 7777 South Lewis Avenue, was such a long drive from town to the campus, to out of town guests and tourists, the drive was always worth it.

I wanted to help people, so I planned to be a missionary or a minister, but when I was caught in another girl's bed, this crazy

Christian college disciplined me so severely, I still have head trauma. I just missed being sent to Conversion Therapy. So I snatched my degree and decided God was over. Evil is always taking care of business so I had to get out there and get busy. Cops are the anointed ones, God's own chosen people, and I was born to be one. I couldn't trust God's judgment, so I joined the police academy where I could be an enforcer. As a cop, I could apply neutral laws to perps. Be an egalitarian. So I became a beat cop, got my degree in CJ from TU, and was set loose on the population. I have a remarkable solve rate because I still have snaps of that divinity I once swallowed without question. So when I care to show that to people, they feel comfortable confessing to me. Fuck God in the eyeball.

CHAPTER SIX

L et's sit in front of the fireplace and eat this while it's hot."
Alistair clapped me on the back. "What do you say, old
sock? There's plenty." Then, to Sophie, "Why don't we have some
wine? God knows you two look positively green."

I gripped my Zippo and took a deep breath to start lining this
joker out. Then I would explain the rules to Sophie. My cell started
ringing. "Excuse me," I said coldly. "Go for Rogers." I watched
Alistair touch Sophie's lower back as they walked toward the living
room together.

"Detective? It's Dana Perryman."

"Sheriff? What can I do for you, doll?" My respect for her grew
because she didn't throw her title around, but I couldn't let her know
that. Yet.

She sighed to ruffle my black flattop. Her voice was a cinder
block. "Rogers, I need you to come to my office."

"Am I in trouble, Barn?"

"You shitty son of a bitch, get your sorry ass in here ASAP!"
Perryman shouted and hung up.

"Lovebirds, I need to reschedule our awkward dinner," I called
into the living room. "Booty call."

Alistair peered around the wall at me. "Certainly, sport." Sophie
emerged, dragging her feet.

"Oh, butter doll, you gonna walk me out?" I bit the words cold and hard like crunching ice.

"Come on, dog in the manger." Sophie took my elbow, propelling me out.

I shook her off. "I don't know that song. Can you sing a little humpin' heifer? Or faithless whore monkey?"

"You drop dead and go to hell." Sophie jerked open the front door and shoved me outside. "Why did you come here?" Sophie hugged herself. The ice pellets fell around us. The wind blew curls out of her braid and across her mouth. I longed to straighten and smooth her hair. I wanted to hold the back of her skull as I crushed her to me in a kiss that would tell her everything.

I would kiss her until she understood. I would make love to that sweet candy mouth, drinking from it until I was intoxicated, feeding her little by little, spark by spark, the torch I had carried all this time until Sophie contained the whole of my blaze. She would glow with my passion. Then when we touched, we would spontaneously combust, flames consuming us both. On my knees, our fires crackling, I would put my mouth on her smoking coal and suck it to cremation. Sophie's cries would rise with the billows of smoke and we would collapse in a pile of ash. Then, from the gray flakes, I would find a chunk of cinder not yet completely incinerated, and I would caress it into ember then to fire then to screaming obliteration. When we were finally, completely cool, the air would turn green and fresh, and Sophie would smile into my face.

I blinked at her. I opened my mouth a couple of times.

"What did you expect?" Sophie's voice was shrill. "Who the hell do you think you are?"

At this point, I knew the questions to be rhetorical so I didn't try to answer.

"I mean, *really*, what is this hot horseshit about you having some harebrained notion with possessiveness? Jill, grow up! And another thing—" Sophie's head started weaving from side to side and she waved a finger in my face. "Don't you *ever* come to my house with a nasty attitude. If you embarrass me again, you'll regret it. Do you understand?"

Sophie stepped out on the stoop to continue her tirade. I backed up, slipping a little. I got the feeling Sophie mastered the impulse to shove me down the stairs. "Just what sort of game did you expect me to play with you? After you snuck out of town without a word like a coward, I'm supposed to stay in the house with my legs closed? I figured I would never see you again. Did you hope my life just stopped?" Sophie acted like she was sniffing me. "God knows *yours* didn't. Did you care for me at all or am I just a port in your lust storm and you're in between docks right now?"

I stumbled back a step. Alistair dashed to Sophie. "Easy, easy, come on in the house." He turned her and they went inside.

The click of the door closing was the worst sound ever. "Ah, fuck," I said. I sat on the step and felt my hope about this place disintegrate. I pulled out my Zippo and clicked it open and closed over and over. Where I had been solid was crumbling to dust. I had not realized how much I had counted on Sophie being mine. I had been biding my time, getting settled in my house, my new job, waiting for the perfect time to present myself. I began shivering, from cold or disappointment; I didn't know and didn't care. My head was pounding. I touched my forehead and felt half a golf ball under my skin. I just wanted to take a minute to gather myself before facing the sheriff. Click open, click closed, click open, click closed.

Behind me, I heard the front door open, and in that uncontrollable split second, my mind pictured Sophie running outside and embracing me, saying all that had been a bad dream and she was crazy about me and that Alistair was her long-lost brother who had been away in England for many years.

Instead, I felt something hot and wet hit my neck. "And clean yourself up! You look like a thug," Sophie said, her voice cracking. I heard Alistair soothing her away from the door, their muffled voices blending before the door shut me in silence again. Just me, the Zippo, the ice, and the collapsing trees.

I lifted the sodden wad of paper towels off my neck—Sophie was a good shot—and I daubed my face and neck. The towels turned red, and I debated about leaving it right where I sat. But that was childish and not the way to a woman's heart. I stood and approached the door, my shoulders slumped, my bravado gone. I knocked.

Alistair opened the door. I handed him the bloody towels, which he graciously accepted.

"Got any aspirin?" I said, then added, "please?"

"Sure, of course. One minute. I can't invite you in because I think she's actually rabid, you understand." He left the door cracked.

I rubbed my hands together and considered my pitiful self. How many new lows could I endure? Waiting on the winter street for my crush's lover to bring aspirin after having been rejected and humiliated and yelled at had to be a fine, fresh low.

"Here you go, old boy. And I'm sorry about it." Alistair handed me a bottle and shut the door.

I dropped six in my mouth and said loudly to the door, "Got any beer?"

This time, Sophie opened the door, her mouth pinched into a line, her face closed, and her eyes flat. "That's all we have. Take care." She handed me a bottle of Guinness.

I should be accustomed to the door shutting in my face, but I wasn't. That impersonal "take care" cut deep. My mouth full of pills, I shouted "Thanks!" at the house. I took a huge swallow and coughed and choked. "Shit! That shit is nasty! Shit!" I shook my head and eased myself back to my car and started driving downtown. I kept the Guinness close.

I parked at the courthouse and found the sheriff's entrance unlocked and took the Guinness inside with me. "Sheriff Perryman? It's Rogers. You here?" My shouts echoed down the long, cold, dark hallway.

I crept cautiously down the hall, cursing myself for not having a flashlight. The Zippo was handy but not bright. *Just like you.* Sophie's voice echoed in my head. "I think I'm hitting all the steps of stupid on the way down. I'm not missing a single one," I said to myself.

"Who's there?" A voice over my right shoulder startled me. I gasped, grabbed my heart, and whirled around. A bit of my Guinness splattered on the wall. "Goddammit, it's me. Who did you think?"

"Who's there?" Perryman squinted. "All I can see is teeth."

"You bitch. What do you want?"

"Come into my office." Perryman turned and went back to her desk.

"Where it's warm and light?" I said.

"Butt in chair, Rogers," Perryman said. She had propped a flashlight on its end inside a ceramic coffee mug, and it flooded the room with eerie, weak light. I heard a bell ringing and an enormous orange tabby cat jumped onto Perryman's desk.

"Fuck!" I said, clutching my chest. "What is that?"

"You're a detective; can't you deduce that he's a cat?" Perryman said.

"Why is it here?"

"Not it. He. His name is Jonathan Bennett and he's here because I like the company."

"Were you raised in a barn? Does the sheriff's office need a good mouser?" The cat swatted his tail with astonishing accuracy and knocked a cup of pencils to the floor.

"All right, enough," Perryman told me. She stroked Jonathan's back. He arched and purred.

"Want me to go milk the cows, Elsie?" I said.

"Knock it off." Perryman glared at me. Jonathan ran across the desk, scattering papers and watching them flutter to the floor. At last, the cat settled on top of Perryman's laptop, tail still swishing and slashing.

"What's that around its, I mean, *his* neck?" I reached for what looked roughly like a flat, black globe about two inches across. Jonathan raised a warning paw the size of a tangerine. I drew back.

"That's a cat cam," Perryman said. "It takes photos while he wears it. I can program it to take them every few seconds or every few minutes. Then I plug it into my computer and see the world from Jonathan's viewpoint. It's really fascinating to see where he goes and what he does."

I laughed derisively. "Oh, I'm *sure.*"

"Sit down. Let's talk business."

I groaned as I eased myself into a chair and propped my feet on her desk. I was glad to be away from Sophie and the pizza of rejection and somewhere more manageable. "What are your turn-ons and turn-offs?"

"That's quite a knot on your head. You talk to somebody besides me today?"

"Lay off."

"Well, I called you here because Jim Harrison is on his way."

I let my booted feet fall to the floor with a thud. "And you needed me here for backup?"

"Looky here what I found by the emergency exit!" A deputy entered with an LED lantern. "Whaddya know about that?" He set it on the desk and waited for responses.

"Thanks, Adams."

"Hey, puddy tat!" Adams stroked Jonathan. "I tell you what, people sure are dumb, you know that?" Adams seated himself next to me and put a pinch of snuff in his cheek. Then he dug through Perryman's trash for a spit cup. He spoke while he sorted through the garbage. "Got a call yesterday. This ole boy has a prize pig and this ole gal who lives next door to him wants to file a protective order against that pig. Heh, heh, heh, heh, heh." Adams sat back, a Styrofoam coffee cup in his hand. "Hey, Peevyhouse, come on in here, boy."

Another deputy entered and leaned against the doorjamb.

"Why the long face, Peeve? Your mama stop puttin' out?" Adams said.

"No, yours did," Peevyhouse said. "Morning, Chief. Hey, kitty, kitty. Who's this guy?"

I assumed he was addressing me rather than Jonathan. "Rogers." Without rising, I shook the deputies' hands. I chose not to correct them about my gender. It really didn't matter. Jonathan, stretching on his side, kicked several files to the floor. His tail flapped madly, almost creating wind.

"Rogers?" Adams spat into his cup. "Rogers with Homicide? You have a rep-you-tation."

I laughed. "Aw, shucks, I just chase people for a living."

"Our jobs are far more involved than that," Perryman said.

"It's actually less so," I said. "Come on, Dana. You know we mostly just sit around and wait for a lucky break. We hang out hoping for tips. That's how cases get solved."

"Don't you *dare*—" Perryman said.

"I heard you was Injun," Adams interrupted, drooling into his cup. "You don't look Injun. How much Injun are ya?"

"You don't look white. How much white are you?"

Adams guffawed. "I only ask cause I'm part Injun too. One of my ancestors was a full-blood princess."

"You don't say!" Peevyhouse said. "You can't swing a dead cat without hittin' Injuns round here. All of 'em drunks with free government handouts. I wish—"

"That's enough!" Perryman barked.

"Did you just come off patrol?" Adams asked Peevyhouse.

"Yeah," Peevyhouse said, removed his hat, brushed it off, and replaced it. "Had to arrest a guy for domestic A&B. Just now dropped him at the jail."

"County has power?" Perryman asked.

"Yeah, they got that emergency generator. They'll be good for a few days," Adams said then chuckled. "Course, I guess we'll have to let them all go free if the power's out for very long."

"That's nonsense, Adams," Perryman said.

"Hey, that perp told me a story. Y'all like good stories? Here goes—you know what all battered women have in common?" Adams said.

"They just won't," Peevyhouse began and then he and Adams finished in unison, "listen!" Then they both laughed. Jonathan sat up and gave us the stink eye.

"Hey, you know what all deputies have in common?" I said.

"Rogers!" Perryman's voice was like a whip crack. "Shut up and I mean it."

"Looks like you in trouble, boy," Adams said.

"Sheriff? I've gotta be somewhere. What did you need?" I asked.

"I have to discuss that case with you. Just give me a minute," Perryman said.

"You hear about the rodeo?" Peevyhouse said.

"They cancelled it cause of the weather, didn't they?" Adams said.

"Yep. I was all set to do my bronc bustin', but they're skipping the whole thing this year."

"Well, you get ice like that outside, you can't transport the bulls. You know what I mean?"

"Boys!" Perryman said. "Ya'll hungry?" I sensed an affected accent had crept into her speech.

"Yes, ma'am, we surely are," Adams said.

"I ain't had no breakfast. You know why?" Peevyhouse said.

"Why?" I said.

"Well, like everything else, my reefer's dead, so I put everything outside so it would stay froze and my hound dogs got loose and ate all my food off my front porch."

"The hell you say!" Adams said. "Them would be some dead dogs if ya ask me."

"They ate my brown and serve sausages, my French toast sticks, my Blue 'n Gold bacon, and a loaf a bread," Peevyhouse said. "I almost ate dog food, but then I thought somebody would have donuts here, but nobody's here and all the donut shops are closed."

"Weeeeelll, that's about as helpful as hen shit on a pump handle, ain't it?" Adams said.

"Mind if I smoke?" I asked.

"Smoke 'em if ya got 'em," Adams said.

"Here's an ashtray." Peevyhouse reached across Perryman's desk and set an object close to me.

"Don't!" Perryman said and tried to grab the ashtray.

"What's this?" I said, lifting the object. "You'll have to develop more skills to be quicker than I, Sheriff." I smiled as if my teeth were coated in mint oil.

"It's not mine," Perryman said. She busied herself giving Jonathan some crunchy treats.

"It was a gift!" Peevyhouse said.

The ashtray was a miniature model of an outhouse. Above the toilet seat was a sign that read: Put yer butts here. "Oh, that's darling." I grinned at Perryman. "Cigarette?" I extended my Camels to her.

"You got any Pell Mells?" Peevyhouse asked. "Them's my favorite."

I shook my head and offered my pack. Peevyhouse waved them away.

"You got any hand-rolled?" Adams said, his cheek bulging with sodden tobacco.

"Naw, but it still smokes good," I said.

"Smoking is against state law. All of you know that," Perryman said.

"Smokin'! This ain't smokin'! This is just a *conference* between *colleagues*," Peevyhouse said, raising his eyebrows on the big words.

"I can wait." I closed my pack and settled myself, clicking my Zippo. With no Sophie to run to, I had all the time in the world.

"Y'all hear about Bo and Skeet?" Peevyhouse stretched, his leather equipment belt creaking agreeably.

"What?" Adams spat into his cup. "About their assignment to the hospital?"

"Yep," Peevyhouse said. "Say, Sheriff, why'd you do that?"

"My decision, Peeve. Better fit," Perryman said coldly.

"What, a couple of miscreants got shunned to pull the crazy criminal guard at Bush Memorial?" I said.

"Why don't ya'll go get some chicken fried steak? I'll buy." Perryman peeled some bills off a roll she had in a drawer. Jonathan immediately tried to fit his great bulk into the open drawer.

"That's mighty white of you," Peevyhouse said, "but no place is open!"

"I bet the grill is open over there by the Y," Adams said. "You ever been there?" he asked me.

"No, is it good?"

"Is it good!" Adams repeated. "It's so good you need a trough and a bib. If you walk away clean, you ain't doin' it right."

"That applies to women as well," I said.

There was silence for two beats and then the deputies howled. Perryman stood and thundered, "Get out! Go to lunch, go on patrol, I don't care. I'm in a meeting."

Adams stood. "Oh, in a meeting, huh? Well, excuuuuuuuuse us." The pair left, laughing.

"Now whatcha got?" I said.

"We wait for him." Perryman shrugged, stroking her cat.

CHAPTER SEVEN

I'm telling you, that woman was murdered!" Sheriff Perryman said after Jim had arrived and sat on the desk, towering over us. Perryman hoped to convince him to file charges on the freeway hit-and-run. I played idly with my lighter, letting her take the lead.

"Why are you even here today, Sheriff?" Jim said. "And what is that animal doing here? You should be at home with your family. Don't worry about such things now. Worry about keeping your kids warm and fed. And keeping filthy animals outside where they belong."

Perryman slapped the top of her desk as she bolted to her feet and put her finger in the DA's face. "Why are you stonewalling me on this?" Jonathan dropped into Perryman's vacated warm and soft chair. He kneaded his claws in the material and I swear it looked as if he were smiling.

"The deputies on the scene say it was just an unfortunate accident." Jim glanced at me and his lip curled. I winked.

"*I* say it was homicide!" Perryman said.

"You've been sheriff for what," Jim looked at his watch, "five minutes now. If you like this job, try to fit in. Don't make waves. Election time will come eventually, and it can be brutal."

Perryman flung Jonathan to the floor and dropped back into her chair, deflated. "You don't *want* to prosecute this case."

Jim grinned and shrugged, holding out his hands. Jonathan rubbed against his legs, leaving fur all over his slacks. Jim shoved the cat away with a grimace and slapped at his pants legs. "What case? There's no case."

"I have my sources who swear it is murder."

Jim laughed. "Sources? Who, this prick?" He jerked his thumb at me.

Perryman blinked. "I thought she was the best."

"I am," I said, but no one was listening. This was Perryman's bullfight.

Jim shrugged again. "She does some good work occasionally. But she makes a lot of mistakes. Rogers is okay if I keep my thumb on her. Otherwise, she runs amok with bizarre conspiracies and amateur theories."

"The hell you say!" I said, but neither of them responded. I decided to pet Jonathan.

"Listen, the husband has no alibi. I know Detective Rogers is right."

"Sheriff, my office is at caseload capacity. We're not equipped to file murder charges based on female intuition."

"You file dog cases all the time! You clog up the court dockets with shit that dead defenders can get dismissed merely to train your newbies. The judges hate you because you waste everyone's time and resources with cases that are tissue thin without probable cause!"

"That's a fact," I said, lighting a cigarette.

"Drop it." Jim reached across Perryman's desk and picked up the lantern. "Accidents happen. I'll see myself out." The light wavered and shadows slid crazily over the walls as he exited, leaving us in the dark.

"Election time will come for you too, asshole!" Perryman called. Then she fell as if dead into her chair. "What now?" Jonathan abandoned my amateur hand and jumped into Perryman's lap.

"You know what," I said.

"We build a case?"

"Bingo."

Chapter Eight

I sat in my idling car with the heat on high, holding my icy Guinness to one of the vents with one hand and smoking with the other. My portable emergency weather radio stated the ice storm had stalled over Oklahoma and that more than an inch of ice had been deposited so far. Trees and power lines were coming down; driving was treacherous; go to one of the local shelters and stay there.

What was the DA up to? I could never finger him. He was pure neo-Christian, right-wing, conservative nutbag, batshit politics, and behind the family values billboard, was as slippery as waxed ice. I needed inside dope. I called my mole, Marny Marlowe, disgruntled ADA.

"Jill! How the hell are you?"

"Worried about that son of a bitch, Marny. How are you?"

"Oh, baby, I'm good. Takin' a tub. What did Jesus Jim do now?"

I heard running water as she turned on the faucet. "He refuses to file a case."

Marny snorted and coughed. "Oh, don't do that when I'm swallowing wine."

"Are you in a bubble bath with candles?" I demanded, blowing smoke out of my cracked car window, watching the gray ice accumulate on my windshield.

"Of course I am. Office is closed today."

"And you're drinking already?" I swigged the last of my Guinness.

"Honey, don't hate. Good Cabs make life worthwhile."

"Like hell. I can't stand Bordeaux."

Marny chuckled. "You just haven't met the right one."

"That's what my mama said about men and look how that turned out."

Marny's throaty laugh made my fingers twitch. I pictured her in the bath—short, wet, curly blue-black hair, heart-stopping Irish green eyes, vampire-white skin all slippery and sudsy, and legs that stretched into next week and flaming straight. Total cock-gobbling dick mitt. I decided to return to Sophie's with my tail between my legs.

"So you want me to look into it?" Marny asked.

"I would never compromise your integrity by asking such a thing," I answered.

"Got it. How's your love life?"

"Shitty. Why? What do you care?"

"Just thought I would get your mind off murder for a minute."

"How's yours?"

Marny laughed again and said, "Frederick, say hello to Jill."

And in the background, I heard a male voice obediently say, "Hello, Jill."

I rolled my eyes. "Oh, for God's sake. That's great. That's just great, you whore."

Marny clucked. "That's your jealousy making you peevish. You need a woman."

"Damn right."

"I know someone."

"Aw, hell no. I'm not going on a blind date."

"Just think about it. She's very sweet. Her name is Penelope. I'll send you her photo."

I sighed. "Well, if she puts out, maybe it will be okay."

"Good. Then it's settled. Now about this other thing."

"Murder made to look like a hit-and-run on Highway Seventy-five."

"I'll let you know, ciao."

I closed my phone, rolled up the window, and carefully stood up and started scraping the ice off the windows.

I pulled up outside Sophie's house and rested my forehead carefully on the steering wheel. Which was worse, going home and being alone in the cold, dark or being the embarrassing third wheel in a romance? "I can't face my house. I just can't," I said, my breath trickling out in hot vapor. I was leaning heavily on the hope that I could trade on the brief shared past of Sophie and me for some goodwill and hang time.

I stood up, full of dread. Two houses down in the middle of the road, a woman, fat with coats and scarves, stood sobbing into a hankie. Because the air was so still and the city so quiet, sound carried abnormally well. I could hear her moaning, "My trees, my trees, my trees."

I knocked on the door that I knew so well. This time Sophie answered with a lemony twist to her mouth.

"I'm older and wiser. May I come in?"

"Drop dead. When I want you, I never see you again, and when I'm unavailable, I can't shake you. I think you have a character flaw."

I glared at her. "Yeah, funny, isn't it?"

"Try not to fuck it up this time." Sophie moved aside to let me pass.

I heard opera in the living room, so I followed the music.

Alistair looked up from a pallet on the floor and smiled. "Well, look who's back!"

"And look who's still here," I said.

"Lighten up, old boy. Have a seat. What are you drinking? Do you like Puccini?"

"Not especially." I cringed when my knees popped as I sat on the couch.

"Neither do I," Alistair whispered. "It was Sophie's idea. How about some Miles?"

"Right on!" I smiled. Alistair changed the music.

Sophie reappeared with a glass that she handed to me. "Every time I see you, you're thirsty." I took the glass and tasted it. Bourbon. Just like before I left. Goddamn her. "Thank you," I said to the fireplace as I stared at the blaze leaping and snapping in the grate.

"We don't have any pizza left. You want a sandwich or something?" Sophie bent over me in concern, her brow furrowed. The modesty of her turtleneck just emphasized the body underneath.

"Come sit down with me, Sugarfoot," Alistair reached for her. Miles's horn wove a slow sex spell. I closed my eyes.

"No, nothing for me."

I heard Sophie sit down on the floor. I opened my eyes. They were reading magazines. Sophie was reading *Adbusters* and Alistair was reading *Glamour.*

"Listen to this rubbish: 'for a better sex life, a woman should just relax and be herself. Tension is a mood killer.' Who is this for?"

"Baby women, darling. Ones who are just forming and have stripper Barbie damage," Sophie said, petting Alistair's head.

"This is Sophie's. I love reading these absurd articles!" Alistair smiled up at me.

"Uh—" I tried to speak, but my voice was latched. I stood up and put my backside to the fire. My mind drifted to the last time I was here and it was summer. Summer so hot it was like putting out matches inside my nostrils to breathe. My body had been oily all the time; my armpits were always slick, my shorts were always funky, my hair greasy. The sun baked, fried, roasted, and burned. The light was too bright, bleaching the color out of life itself and pressing on my skin like a scorched iron. I sweated myself dehydrated and never completely cooled down, even in the shower, in air-conditioning, or at night. But how I had loved every minute of that summer. That summer when I met Sophie for the first time. The summer that Sophie bewitched me, the summer of loss and discovery.

The summer I was on the rebound and completely burned out. I fell hard and fast for Sophie when I saw her at Whole Foods, wandering the supplements aisle with her net bag, sundress, and sandals. But it wasn't enough to heal me. I had four murder books on my desk, all stuck in the muddy morass of hopeless dead ends, and I had just broken up by mutual agreement with a woman I had been with for five years. We had just run out of gas. Neither one of us cared anymore, but under pressure, I had promised to remain friends even though I was indifferent to that too.

Chief St. John saw the circles under my eyes, my weight loss, my apathy to interviewing witnesses who had already given statements a dozen times, and he sent me away.

The chief and I have a contentious but affectionate relationship, and I get away with more than I should, but when he issues a command, I have no choice. Because I was embarrassed and ashamed, I left town without a word after a three-month torrid affair with Sophie. I packed and slunk out of town, driving north to South Dakota to stay with very distant relatives on a res.

I stayed in touch with the chief, but I couldn't overcome my shame to contact Sophie.

The summer of glossy golden hair and pink skin and tart raspberry nipples and stolen caresses as sweet as feather honey. Breasts as heavy as heat, triangle of curly crimson fire, hypnotizing me into syrupy stupidity. Opening her legs to find the sweet lava that melted me. I could feel my temperature rising just remembering. Hotter, hotter, and hotter still. The regret boiling in me like acid.

"What's that smell?" Alistair wrinkled his nose.

"You're on fire!" Sophie said, slapping the backs of my legs. I whirled and saw my Burberry scarf—a gift from a woman—ablaze.

"Shit!" I said with disgust, hitting the flames.

"Bad luck," Alistair said.

"Come with me," Sophie said and dragged me into the kitchen. She threw the scarf in the sink and turned on the cold water. "First, are you all right?" The scarf hissed and smoked.

"Yeah, don't get in a lady wad. I'm fine." I turned off the water.

Sophie stared at the backs of my legs. "Your jeans have singe holes in them. Are you sure you're not burned?" She raised her gaze, full of worry, to search my face.

"Yeah, I'm burned," I said, holding her stare until the air started to prickle.

"Hm, well, I'm sorry about that. We're definitely throwing this away." Sophie wrung out the scarf and dropped it into the trash.

"Hey, what's up?" I grabbed her by the shoulders.

Sophie's eyes darkened. "What do you mean?" she asked coolly.

"Cut the shit. You know what I'm talking about." I jerked my thumb at the living room. "That Brit twit."

"Don't do that," Sophie said.

"What's the story? You suddenly got a yen for prick?"

"I'm telling you for the last time, be civil or get out."

"I'm hurt! I'm outraged!"

"That's your problem."

"Tell me why. Can you do that at least?"

"*At least?*" Sophie said. "At *least?* Look where you are standing! Might I remind you, Jill Rogers—"

"All right, all right," I said, waving my hands. "I'm sorry. Would you please tell me?"

Sophie regarded me for a moment and puffed air from her nostrils like a horse. "Sure. It's no secret. I just follow the pleasure." She shrugged. "And I can get pleasure from anyone, man or woman. Pleasure isn't limited to one gender or one type of experience. Pleasure—"

"Oh, give me a break. I am going to vomit."

"Suit yourself."

I glared at her. I wanted to knock her down. I wanted to fuck her. "Why him?"

"What difference does it make? Pleasure is pleasure."

"Stop saying that! It makes everyone sound so…interchangeable."

"And so they are," Sophie said smoothly. "Pleasure—"

"You say pleasure one more time and I'll choke you." I flexed my hands.

Sophie stepped close to me, lifted her chin, and whispered, "Pleasure."

I could smell her perfume. Quick as lightning, I embraced her and slammed my mouth on hers. Her mouth received me hungrily, and we kissed like starved tigers, tearing at each other, panting, clawing, pressing hard, trying to merge our bodies like our mouths, deeper and deeper, getting lost in the spiral.

I heard footsteps, broke the kiss, and moved away. Sophie looked wild and disheveled; I assumed I was a mirror image, so I stared outside, pretending indifference. The ice continued pecking at the windows.

"All right then?" Alistair said, glancing at us and getting a Guinness out of the dark fridge.

"Yes," Sophie said. "Yes. Jill's just," Sophie tenderly daubed her lips, "Jill needs a new scarf."

"Pity," Alistair said and grinned. "Mmm, chilly in here. Come back to the fire."

I faced Sophie without any sex filters. Just one hundred percent smoking desire. I rasped, "Why him?"

Sophie smiled a hideous, sardonic grimace, "'cause he didn't run away when he wanted me."

I closed my eyes. "Gotcha." I walked out of the kitchen through the living room, and out the front door where I stood on the stoop, thunderstruck. "This can't be," I said. I tilted my head back and yelled so loud my feet almost left the ground.

Sophie and Alistair came running.

"Your car!" Sophie said.

"A hit-and-run," I said, my mouth full of vinegar.

"Oh, bloody hell," Alistair clapped me on the shoulder. "Steady on."

"Can't you get one of those unmarked departmental cars or something?" Sophie said.

"I'll try," I said miserably. Alistair went back inside. I dialed the motor pool. A recorded voice told me they were closed indefinitely. I called the emergency number.

"Whitman."

"Rogers here. My car is totaled. What can I get?"

A laugh that turned into a long, rattling hack. "Ain't you heard? We're in the middle of an act a God. Ain't no cars comin' or goin'."

My throat squeezed. "Nothing at all?"

"Jilldo, even if I wanted to, which I *don't*, I couldn't get anything to you. There's a foot of ice on everything. Plus then there's the frozen and powerless electric fence that can't move an inch. I only came in to do payroll for my people. I'm sittin' in my parka in the cold dark down here. You'll have to stay put."

Without a further word, I ended the call and shrugged.

"You'll never get a tow. Want to stay here?" Sophie asked softly.

Chapter Nine

My phone rang immediately. "Rogers!" I shouted into the phone, hoping whoever was on the other end would say something stupid.

"Rogers, Perryman. I found something."

I grinned. "Hey, foxy. What you know good?" I noticed Sophie watching me, and I was filled with giddy satisfaction. I turned and left the room after I wolf-winked at Sophie.

Down a long, dark hallway and out of earshot, I leaned wearily against the wall, my whole body sagging. I put a hand over my eyes and my voice changed. "Okay, Sheriff. What have you found?"

"Can you come to the evidence room?"

My throat was powdery with bitterness, but I laughed. "Nope. I'm stuck. My car is totaled."

"Hm. That presents a problem."

"Little bit."

"Well, can I come there?"

"Not a good idea. I'm not at home."

"What then?"

"Sheriff, I really can't worry about this now. I will contact you as soon as I have wheels."

"Borrow my car." The voice was liquid satin floating out of the darkness and wrapping me in snaps of electricity. Barely visible was a shadow darker than the dark: Sophie.

"What?" I said.

"With me in it," she continued, all ripply ripe.

"I'll see you in ten." I told Perryman and hung up. "Soapytoes, just what do you think you're doing?"

She took a step closer. "I'm stir crazy and want to get out."

"So take a walk around the block."

She stepped closer. I could see her face a little now. "I've done that. I want to get…" Sophie stepped closer, "farther," and closer, "out." When she stopped, our feet were touching.

I cupped her jean-clad cunt and whispered, "There will be none of this."

Sophie nodded.

"Or this." I rolled my thumbs over her sweater. I felt two BBs rise to the surface.

"I know."

"Or this." I knocked her head back and bit her throat.

"Definitely not," Sophie moaned.

My mouth, pulsing with heat, hovered above her ear that was covered in loose vanilla curls. "No foolishness," I breathed, running my hands slowly down her sides and finally taking possession of her round ass. I clutched and squeezed it like a crash victim with an airline seat. Sophie closed her eyes and leaned against the wall, raising her pelvis to me.

"Absolutely," Sophie whispered, her mouth swollen and succulent.

I stood erect, put my hands in my pockets, shaking the spell. Curiously, Sophie's desire helped me have strength to set mine aside.

"But, Jill, what about this?" Sophie pulled my mouth back to hers. I sank into that sensual madness and devoured her for all the years of denial, for all the fantasies, for the unknown future when I probably would never get it again. Her arms locked me close, and her leg curled around to hold me. Sophie's moans made my entire body ache with desire. My wrists, my vertebrae, my feet, my hips throbbed with pain, needing this woman. Her panting told me she had wanted me for a very long time too.

I was an expert at women's voices, and this desire wasn't fresh. Sophie's desire for me was aged and bittersweet with unrequited misery. I imagined her, after I left for South Dakota, injured and unfulfilled, replaying our few moments together with an intensity that would keep her wanting. I pictured her, night after night, falling back into bed, panties off, eyes closed, legs wide, gasping for relief, wishing me there, her whole body twitching in agony for me. For my brown hands to stroke and soothe her, for my tongue to tenderly caress satisfaction into her cunt, for her to scream my name, claw my flesh to bloody ribbons as her passion is finally sated. For me to fill her up, expanding, side to side, up and down, front and back until her distress melted into contentment.

But I hadn't been there to do that. Sophie had simmered and seethed, restless with torment, month after month, until now with my mouth on hers, these moans rising up from the basal core of her, confessing everything.

I pulled on her braid, jerking her head back. I stared at her, her eyes famished for me, her mouth carnivorous and wet. I knew she wanted me to make a scene. To demand she break up with Alistair, to beg for status, to plead with her for another chance, to tell her all I would do for her. To make forever promises. But I didn't. I simply met her stare. My hands were shaking so I folded my arms across my chest, separating us. "No, there will be none of that either," I said softly, then called, "Alistair!" Sophie's eyes widened and she shook her head. "Wanna go for a ride?" I yelled. Sophie hissed at me and stormed into the kitchen, smoke trailing after. I heard glass breaking. I figured Sophie threw the empty soldiers too hard into the recycling.

"I ain't playin' that," I said, walking to the living room. Sophie was already there, facing the fire, staring at the flames. Alistair was sipping his Guinness.

"Count me out. I'm just ducky right here. This weather is not my cuppa. But maybe Sophie? Sugar, you want to go?"

"No, I'll stay here," Sophie said. She was too quiet.

"Okay, keys?" I clapped and rubbed my hands together briskly.

"In here." Sophie led me to her bedroom, her face impassive. She refused to look at me. She rummaged in her purse. "Here, you lousy son of a bitch." Sophie hurled the keys into my belly and there was a bloom of pain and a burst of fury in my head. I leaped on her and we fell onto the bed.

I straddled Sophie's body and gripped her arms, shaking her. "What's your problem, huh? What is wrong with you?"

Sophie did not answer. Her eyes were dilated and dark. I saw two tears slide out of the edge of each eye and fall to the bed. Sophie screwed up her mouth and spit in my face, her neck straining. She looked like a cobra. My hand flew into the air as a reflex, and before I could dislocate her jaw with my backhand, I froze. I left my hand poised in the air and closed my eyes and breathed.

Sophie didn't make a sound. When I finally looked at her, her face was radiating such sadness and desire that I lowered my hand inch by inch by inch by inch. I just sat back and drank in the delicious sight of her. Without a sound, I crouched lower and lower toward Sophie's lips. Lower. Lower still. Almost there. Our eyes locked. Lower. Lower. Finally, I closed my mouth gently over hers. Her breath filled my lungs.

Our union was as soft as I could make it. I channeled my former rage into restrained longing. With my kiss, I tried to tell her I was sorry. My mouth told her how much I regretted the loss and how right she was. I kissed. I kissed her as if she were disintegrating; I kissed mercy into her mouth. I kissed her so tenderly and so slowly, my eyes filled with water. I kissed as if my mouth were fragile; I kissed her until there was peace between us. I kissed her until Sophie was settled but before the passion could build. When I finally stood, my limbs were singing with honey. I picked up the keys off the floor and left the house.

Chapter Ten

Outside, the ice grains were still falling. Underfoot, it was thick and white like snow. I looked at my sorry car. The fender was knocked clean away and had skidded down the street to rest in the gutter. The trunk was crumpled like an accordion almost to the backseat. The trunk lid was open and folded in half. I hefted the garage door open, grunting as I rolled it up on its tracks. Wouldn't you know, Sophie owned a Volvo station wagon. I got in, started the car, and let it warm up. I walked back out to the street to retrieve my sad fender. There was a boy with mean eyes leaning against a tree smoking a cigarette.

I nodded to him as I lifted the fender out of the gutter. "Whassup, baby man?"

"Pops."

"What?"

"Call me Pops. Got another smoke?" Pops finished that cigarette and flicked it into the ice where it sizzled.

I laughed. "No, I don't, not for you. Why don't you go home and have a glass of milk or go sledding?" Pops stared at me, his gaze slicing me like razors. And there was no contempt sharper than that of the young for the old. "How old are you?"

"Ten."

"Jesus, Mary, and Joseph, boy, get your ass off this street corner and stop actin' a fool. Where's your mama?"

"Nunya."

"What?"

"*None of your business.*"

I wanted to box his ears. "Go on now. Quit hanging. Realize your potential."

"I saw who did that." Pops said and then grinned when he noticed my expression.

I lowered the fender to the ground. "Well?" I said.

Pops scratched his chin as if deciding whether to give me the job. "I can't concentrate unless I'm smoking."

I laughed. "Good try. See you around." I picked up the fender and began walking away.

"Wait! Okay. You have a good face."

"I have a good badge too."

"It was a white guy in a white Escalade."

"Uh huh." I was stony. "That it?" I walked a few more steps, the ice crunching underfoot.

"It had a sign on the back."

I turned, the fender swinging a wide arc with me. "Spill, Pops."

"One of those crazy fish."

"All right." My bladder shriveled with dread. "Follow me." I walked to my car and perched the fender in the backseat, leaving it jutting out of the window. Then I went to Sophie's Volvo, opened the passenger door, and said to Pops, "Hop in." I walked to the driver's side and sat. I turned the heater on high and rolled down the windows. I withdrew two American Spirit cigarettes, taken off a date's nightstand weeks ago, put them in my mouth, and with my Zippo, lit both and handed one to Pops.

"What the hell is this?" Pops said.

"Kool-Aid," I answered, my cigarette bobbing up and down with my words, "whaddya think?"

"I'm not blowing a blunt with a pig."

I held the cigarette and said, "three...two..."

Pops snatched it and inhaled.

I put the car in reverse and said, "You've got a real problem, Pops."

He cackled. "You have no idea, sir."

I drove downtown, and Pops never asked where we were going or why. When I pulled up at the sheriff's office, he glared. "Hey, you can't arrest me!"

"Relax. I just have to go in for a minute. You coming?"

"Aw, what the hell."

We both finished our smokes simultaneously. I knew Sophie would go bitchcakes if I left tobacco in her car, so I held my hand out to Pops. He didn't understand. I ground my butt in the palm of my heavy leather glove. There were scorch marks from previous emergency ashtray situations. Pops shook his head, his eyes wide. I grabbed his butt and ground it out for him. I closed my fist and nodded. We got out and Pops promptly lost his footing and fell on his rear.

"I'm all right," he said, turning pink.

We walked into the building. "Oh, shit, I forgot my flashlight again." I slapped the wall.

"I got one." Pops's childish voice echoed down the dark hallways. He fumbled in his jacket pocket and produced a tiny penlight. "Better than nothing," he said defensively.

I called Perryman to find out where she was. I hung up and said, "To the basement."

"We're not going to see anything dead, are we?" Pops's voice seemed so young and tiny. I wanted to hug the fake adult out of him and start him over in babyhood.

"No," I said, not sure myself. We saw a head lamp glowing in the distance and followed that to the evidence room.

"What is this place?" Pop whispered.

"A place I want you to forget immediately," I said. "Sheriff," I greeted Perryman.

"Rogers," Perryman said, momentarily blinding me with her headlamp when she turned to face us. "Sorry," she adjusted the beam, "who's the kid?"

"Came with the car."

"Look at this!" Perryman picked up a cardboard box.

"Pops, why don't you go sit over there?" I pointed to a desk in the corner. "I won't be long." Pops shone his miniature light and wandered to the corner.

"What are you doin' down here in the evidence room?" Deputy Harris startled us. Pops kept his mouth shut.

"None of your business, Harris," said Perryman. "What do you need?"

"We got some warrants we need you to sign off on. Shouldn't take a minute. Then you can get back to your snoopin'." Harris stepped closer and examined the name written on the boxes. "If you just come with me, we can git 'er did."

"Harris, let Lane do the warrants. And you get back out on patrol."

"But Lane—"

"I don't care. A dozen other deputies can do the warrants. I'm busy."

"I believe that case is closed." Harris pointed with his chin at the boxes. "Hit-and-run."

"Not the way I see it," I said.

"I agree with Rogers." Perryman drew herself tall.

"You would think the high sheriff would be concerned with unsolved, open cases instead of wasting tax payers' dollars over a plunk. And blowing the city's time and money too." He gestured to me.

"I don't think this is a waste of time, and I am not putting any manpower on it. I'm merely poking around."

Harris shrugged and sighed loudly. "Well, excuses are like buttholes; everybody has one."

I laughed. Harris glanced at me.

Perryman set her jaw and stared him down, saying nothing. Finally, Harris adjusted his leather equipment belt. "Well, all right, then. Guess I'll go on."

"You like kids, Harris?"

"Ma'am?" Puzzled, Harris glanced in confusion at Pops, who sat silently in the shadows.

"Do. You. Like. Children?"

"Much as the next one, I reckon."

"You behave that way to me again, you'll be on crosswalk duty until you die."

Harris pursed his lips, rolling retorts in his mouth, but swallowing them. He removed a snuff box from his pocket and made a great show of extracting a pinch, opening his stained, snaggle-toothed maw, and tucking the tobacco inside. "Sheriff, I'm headed out on patrol."

"Good man." Perryman turned back to the evidence box and lifted the boots the victim's husband had been wearing the night of her death. She handed me a boot. "Look at this!"

I took it. "Is this what I'm looking for? These sticky boogers deep in the waffle tread?"

Pops laughed. "Boogers."

"Yes, the residue."

"Yep, it's there. Good catch, Sheriff. There is monkey business somewhere. What are you going to do now?"

"What does it mean?"

"I don't know, but it's suspicious. Get a search warrant somehow. Subpoena his phone records and bank statements. Talk to his insurance agent. One rule for every crime—follow the sex and money." I handed the boot back to Perryman. "I'd like to be there when you interview him. C'mon, Pops!" The penlight bounced as Pops jumped from the desk and ran to my side.

In the parking lot, I gestured to the white Escalade with the Christian fish symbol on the back. "A car like that?" I asked Pops.

His eyes widened. "Yes, sir!"

I checked the front of the vehicle—minor denting and paint transfer. "Damn Jim to hell," I said.

When we were in the car returning home, I glanced at Pops. His right arm was propped against the door with his thumb in his mouth. His head leaned against the side of the car and his eyes were half-open and glazed with sleep. A section of his hair was pasted straight up against the glass.

When we got back to Sophie's, I didn't want to wake him, so we stayed in the car together. I parked in the sun in the driveway and left the motor running so the heat would stay on. I leaned my head back and closed my eyes too.

Chapter Eleven

Okay, we're here with Rick Goodson to interview him about his wife's death. It's December twelfth, seven p.m. I am Sheriff Perryman, and this is Detective Rogers who will be observing. Can we get you anything?"

The man sitting at the interview table was fidgety but using all his energy to conceal it. He was lean with thinning, sandy hair, and a righteous jaw. Perryman had insisted on bringing in a generator for this interview so she could have lights and the camera and voice recorder without having to mess with batteries. When she called me at Sophie's to tell me the suspect was cooperative and on his way in, I asked how she had gotten him to agree.

"Just asked if he wouldn't mind helping."

"Little lady in over her head and the big, strong suspect swoops in to straighten everything out?"

Perryman laughed, delighted with herself. "Poor little old me. I just can't make heads or tails of all these confusing reports with this pretty bonnet on. Now get in here, Rogers."

The suspect looked at each of us. "I thought this was all settled already. The ME confirmed it was an accident." Rick drummed his fingers on the tabletop, caught himself, pulled his hands to his lap, started popping his knuckles, caught himself, and stopped. "Can I get some water?"

Perryman nodded at me. "Sure. Rogers will be right back with that."

When I returned to the room, I held the cup out, and when Rick reached for it, I raised it above his head. "What happened to your hand, Mr. Goodson?"

"Oh that," he said and laughed. "Dog bite."

"What were you doing that a dog bit you?" I grabbed his hand and stared at the injury. "That is pretty severe. It looks infected. You want to be careful of blood poisoning so if you start getting red streaks on your skin, run, don't walk to the ER." I handed him the water.

"Were you cheating on your wife, Mr. Goodson?" Perryman asked. His eyes went tree frog and he put the water cup to his mouth and drank and drank, as if it were fiery August. I looked at Perryman and winked; she rolled her eyes. Still the suspect drank. I looked at my watch. Perryman yawned. She tapped a neat stack of papers into a neater pile. Still he drank. I scratched my scalp, thinking about needing a haircut. Perryman picked her nails. I gingerly touched the bump on my forehead. Perryman rattled change in her pocket. I removed my pistol from its holster and set it on the table pointing the muzzle at Rick.

"I don't think there's *that* much water in that cup," I said, flipping my Zippo.

Rick set the cup down, panting. "I'm just very thirsty lately. Maybe I am getting an infection. Now what's this all about? I need to go home to be with my kids."

"Just routine. A few questions came up and we wanted to completely eliminate you as being involved, so we really appreciate your help. I know that's what you want too," Perryman said.

"Yes, yes, of course. Any way I can be of help."

"So there's nothing you haven't told us?" Perryman paged through the report. "You have nothing further to add?"

"No, nothing. Why? Has something happened?"

"Well, since you have nothing to hide, you won't lawyer up?" I asked. "Only guilty people need attorneys," I added. Then I spun the gun on the table. "You don't need one, do you?" The gun stopped, the barrel pointing at Rick again.

"You've been Mirandized," Perryman cut in, "so we will respect your wishes, Mr. Goodson. Do you want to talk to us?"

"Do you want to *help?*" I said.

Rick glared at me and then smiled at Perryman. He repeated, "Yes, of course. Anything I can do. How can I help? But this has to be quick. I need to get back to my children."

"Certainly, sir." Perryman sat down and said warmly, "My own kids are grown. How old are your babies, Mr. Goodson?"

"Eighteen and seventeen."

I stood up, grabbed my gun, and went to lean in the corner.

"Oh, I think your children will be okay for a little bit," Perryman said.

"Well, my mother is with them."

"What's the matter with your face, Mr. Goodson?" I said.

"Huh? Nothing."

"You've got pancake on there thick as frosting. Are you a cross-dressing lounge singer?"

"What? No, I'm…I just…"

"We want to *help* you, sir," Perryman said. Then she squinted and made a move to touch his face but pulled back. "Is it…some sort of sunscreen? Or a kind of medicine maybe?" Her smile sparkled.

"Well…no, not really."

"Are you a transvestite? Is that the problem? Lord!" I yelled. "Do your children know? Does your pastor?" I sounded like Foghorn Leghorn.

"Rogers! Cool it!" Perryman ordered.

"I think you're on the down low and we caught you mid-makeover before you could catch your dates on the stroll."

"*What!* Just what is this? What does my face have to do with my wife's accident?"

"Plenty," I said. "Go wash your face." I was breaking all my rules, but I couldn't help it. This guy brought out the hammer in me. My interrogation rules were simple, but very difficult: lying is cooperative, so be easy and agreeable. Don't push; don't be brutal; that's for amateurs and television. Pack away the testosterone and the competitive desire to win. The aim wasn't domination or terror or even being right, the goal was an airtight confession. And for me, those never happened under stress or threat. I tried breathing to calm down, but I just ending up angrily gasping though clenched teeth.

"Could you see your way clear to go rinse your face, Mr. Goodson, sir? Just so you won't distract Rogers anymore. Be a big help."

I strode to the other side of the room, my gun back in its holster, my head down, arms crossed over my chest. "Sink's here," I said as I kicked open the bathroom door that was attached to the interview room.

"Thanks," Rick said faintly.

Perryman and I started whispering once we heard the water running. "You got a search warrant?" I said.

"Yeah, Judge Williams is a neighbor. I drew up a PC affidavit and he signed, no problem. I've got some men at his place now."

"Way to go, Sheriff," I clapped her on the back, "how long before he bolts?"

Perryman shrugged. "I am surprised he stayed this long. I would've gone a long time ago."

"Me too. I would've had the most expensive attorney tell us to fuck off."

The water stopped. Rick emerged, daubing his face with paper towels. I cocked my head like a dog. "What the hell happened to you? Did you cut yourself shaving?"

Rick's face was covered in angry red claw marks. "No." He was sullen. "I was out hiking and fell into some briars."

"You want to try again?" I said. "You're killin' me! I've heard better lies from a six-year-old. That wound on your hand is a fight bite. I'd know it anywhere. The human mouth is lousy with germs. And those kisses on your face are from your dearly departed wife. Am I right?" I put a foot on the table, hovering over him.

"Those do look pretty serious. Have you seen a doctor?" Perryman added.

Rick swallowed, picked up the empty water cup, stared into it, put it down, and said, "I'm ending this interview. I want a lawyer."

"Damn right." I patted his shoulder.

"Okay, this concluded the interview with Mr. Rick Goodson on December twelfth, seven thirty p.m. Thank you for coming in, sir. We'll be in touch."

"What she means is, we are releasing you for now, but do not leave town," I said.

Rick stared hate at us and left.

"Low five," I said, holding my hand stretched down by my hip. Perryman tickled my palm with her fingers.

I grinned and returned to Sophie's Volvo. The ice had stopped and the clouds were thinning. My phone rang. "Rogers."

"I've got some info for you." Silken voice caressing my ear.

"Ms. Marny Marlowe! Took you long enough! What you know good, girl?"

"I know that you better back off your prime suspect. He's a friend of Jesus Jim's. Charges will not be filed."

"We'll see about that."

"And I have Penelope here. She wants to talk to you."

"Oh, for God's sake, Marny, give me a break." I parked at Sophie's and let myself in. I went to the kitchen where Alistair was staring dreamily into the ice chest on the floor.

"Quite ironic," he said, scooping a handful of ice into a highball tumbler. I laughed, picked up a Guinness, and returned to the living room where Sophie and Alistair were playing cards by battery lantern.

"Come on, just give it a chance," Marny said.

"Fine, put her on."

"Hello?" a bright pink baby voice greeted me.

"Hello, Penelope, sweet thing." My voice was rough as asphalt. I saw Sophie glance at me, frowning.

"Hi! Marny has told me so much about you. And she showed me your photo from last year's police calendar."

"Oh, no," I said, "not that!" I had been coerced into posing on a police horse for a good cause and I had almost shat myself in fear. "That was a bad picture."

"You look real good to me."

"Well, you seem fun too," I said.

Penelope giggled. "I can be…with the proper person."

"Is that right?" I slumped in the couch, swigging the Guinness, then nestling the bottle in my crotch, beginning to like this girl. Sophie was fumbling with the cards, dropping a few. Having trouble shuffling. "So you want to meet and see if we can get some fun started?"

More giggling. "Sure."

"I'll call you, okay, baby?"

Sophie flipped some cards and they whirled across the rug.

"Okay." Penelope replied. Then a breathy giggle. "Bye bye."

Sophie asked, "Who was that?"

"Just a friend of the family," I said and winked, hating my smarmy assholiness but unable to stop.

"Really?"

"Yeah, I think she was a Miss Universe or something."

"How dear," Sophie said with a twist of lime.

"Yeah, so I'll need some fresh sheets, okay?"

"The hell you will." Sophie snapped.

"Sophie!" Alistair said. "What the bloody hell is wrong with you?" He gathered the cards and put them in the box.

"Nothing. I'm going to bed." Sophie announced and caressed Alistair's leg. "You coming?"

"Love to, old girl, but it's only eight p.m."

Sophie mimicked Alistair. "What the bloody hell does that have to do with anything?" She stood with her hands on her hips.

Alistair made a face and rolled his eyes to me. "We have a guest. It's a bit rude, don't you think?"

"Jill?" Sophie snorted. "Jill's no *guest*. She's—"

"That's fine." I cut Sophie off before she could get warmed up. "You two kids go on to bed. Please."

"Sweet bits, you toddle on, get it warm, and I'll be there presently, all right?" Alistair stood and kissed Sophie on the forehead.

Sophie threw her hands in the air. "I give up! I just can't get laid no matter what I do!" She stalked off into the dark and slammed the bedroom door.

Alistair turned, sat on the couch, and said, "Right." He held his Guinness in the air. "Women, eh?"

"Amen, brother." We clicked bottles.

Two hours and many drinks later, I liked Alistair just fine. He was a barrister with the Crown Court in London and was on leave to teach a law class as TU. We were breathless with laughter over a story he was finishing.

"I thought he meant something else entirely when he said he killed over a little tail!" Alistair repeated, snorting with laughter.

I was prostrate on the couch, holding my belly. "Turns out," my voice went falsetto; "he *had* a little tail! Oh, God, oh God!"

Alistair was gasping. "A wee vestigial tail caused him to murder three people!"

"Oh...oh..." I wiped my eyes. "That's prime. Dig this: there was a defendant in our court recently who we picked up in error. Mistaken identity. However, he confessed and was sent to prison. But the fuckup was discovered and he was released. His attorney asked him why he made a false admission, and the defendant said, I kid you not, 'I know a good deal when I see one.'"

"Hoo, hoo, hoo, hoo!" Alistair laughed. "Brilliant. One of the last cases I handled involved the very complex 'Liar, Liar, Pants on Fire' defense."

I was doubled over and slapping the coffee table. "Aw, shit! Get this—these two douchebags I arrested for murder had rolled the victim in an Oriental rug and referred to her in code as 'The Burrito.'"

"What was your first time like?" Alistair asked, suddenly sober.

"My first time…what?" My voice was small and dry and I was wondering how I would describe vag on vag action.

"Seeing one."

"Seeing one what?"

"A body."

I sighed loudly with relief and clicked my Zip open and closed. "Why?"

"I've never seen one and I doubt I ever will." Alistair shrugged.

"Okay…it was ten years ago." I lapsed into silent reflection. I had been a brand-new detective on the homicide team, a newborn arrogant asshole, ready to solve everything and save the world in one day. We walked into a stabbing scene, and I just made it outside before I threw up. When I got home eighteen hours later, I packed up my girlfriend's shit and kicked her out. I swore to myself that the two incidents were not related. But I had to choose one: murder or love, and the choice was clear. Murder was easy. Fuck God in the eyeball. "It was no biggie." I kicked off my boots. "It was a homeless guy, frozen to death under a bridge. We just had to investigate to ensure no foul play. Other than him not having adequate shelter, there wasn't any."

Alistair nodded. "Were you in shock?"

I laughed derisively. "No way. I'm no pussy." I had curled into a fetal ball on the stripped bed and rocked to sleep after crying myself empty and wondering if I could make a living selling shoes. But the sunrise woke me up. I had nowhere else to go. And a desk waiting with my name on it. So I stood up and went back into the office without eating or showering. Chief grinned and slapped me on the back and said it was all normal. "One of the first things I learned was how to collect the dots before connecting the dots. My chief told me that cops are like creditors. Someone has to pay and we always get paid."

Alistair yawned. "Good theory."

"And this ice bugs the shit out of me because everything is so fucking quiet. Just like a massive homicide scene. Murder scenes are always silent. Eerie. Just like this town right now."

"Is that so?"

"Also, in case you're looking to kill someone, a small caliber gun is almost always fatal. Forget those cannons; get something small."

"I'm English. I have no idea what that means."

"Just as well."

"One time—" Alistair broke off and stared into the darkness. "Many apologies, love, are we disturbing you?"

I squinted through the waning candlelight and saw that irresistible silhouette. The silhouette that contained an infinite universe of joy within its curves. The curve of her arched foot like a bridge between the past and the future, cradling the whole of her on its back. The curve of her calf like all the explosive potential stored in the plump battery of her leg. The curve of her sighing thigh like the sacred engine that women have borne for all eternity. The wonder and nourishing meat of that thigh. The curve of her skull, like a dish of stars in the void, the curve of her eyes—seeing and seen in one complete sweetness, the curve of her nose like life itself. Breath embodied. The curve of her cheeks like plums, the curve of her mouth like eternal laughter. The curve of her chin like a cool, clean cliff. The curve of her throat encircling her voice, the curve of her shoulders like polished marble, the curve of her arms like Saturn's rings, dangerous but breathtakingly beautiful, the curve of her hands like the curve of water over a stream bed, the curve of her breasts heavy with smothering abundance that as children of God, we all crave in our cells, the curve of her waist like the speed of light bent around an hourglass, the curve of her belly like a happy puppy, the curve of her buttock like a curl of creamy butter, the curve of her cunt, ah, the event horizon trembling around the ultimate euphoric death. And all her tiny curves—the rind of her heels, the grins of her fingernails....

"No," Sophie answered, "I just came to...to...check my hearing."

The curves of her ears like bells. "Your hearing is fine," I assured her. "Go back to sleep." I enjoyed ordering her to bed as if we were a couple and it was my place to do so. Sophie nodded and returned to her bedroom without another word. She was so ripe for me! So ready to be mine, *mine!* And here sat the reason she's not. Not Alistair, me. Fool.

The atmosphere between Alistair and me had cooled and become awkward. We looked at each other and then back at the fire.

"You think you have enough blankets?" Alistair said.

"Sure."

"We kill the fire, so sleep as you are or you'll get cold fast."

"Right on."

"I forgot to ask, how do you know Sophie?"

Suddenly, I was so tired. I began gathering and straightening blankets.

"Friend of your mum's?" Alistair asked.

"Yeah, that about sums it up."

Alistair nodded silently, just like Sophie. A nod full of thought and truth. "Good night. We'll knock you up about six, all right?"

"Great. Thanks for letting me bunk here."

Late in the night, I woke with a start from a light, busy sleep. My mind was cranking and insomnia was a way of life for me. I just needed to think, and I did my best thinking in the bathroom. I got my cigarettes, flashlight, and lighter and headed quietly to the shitter.

I took my pants off and perched the flashlight next to me, pointing toward the ceiling. I got comfortable and started my first smoke. I let my mind go. I could trust it. It led me to countless good hunches and lucky breaks. I dropped my roach into the water and I flushed the toilet and lit my second cigarette. I was getting cold, but it wasn't time to go back to bed yet. I wished I had thought to drag a blanket in here with me. I kept my knees wide and flicked ashes into the bowl.

The door opened and Sophie clapped her hands to her face. "My eyes!" she cried, "oh, my God, my eyes!"

"Shut up and get out!" I threw one of my boots at her.

Sophie backed out, closing the door. "Stay in there as long as you need. I'll just pee the bed."

I didn't stand up until dawn. I was chilled, my legs stiff, but my mind was clear.

Chapter Twelve

There!" Perryman whispered, holding the binoculars out to me. Rick Goodson, carrying trash bags, emerged from the shadows at the side of his home and placed the trash on the curb. He looked up and down the street warily and then returned to the house. "What time do you make it, Detective?"

"Four a.m."

"And why would you ever put your garbage at the curb at such an hour unless you were hiding something? Why not set it out yesterday evening like everyone else?"

The neighborhood had optimistically lined the street with trash carts and bags, hoping life to be normal.

"And the trucks will be running later because of the ice," Perryman added.

"If they're even working, I haven't heard."

"Exactly." Perryman let the unmarked patrol car creep up to the trash bags. "Now go to the trunk," Perryman pulled the lever to pop the trunk lid, "and put the sacks of garbage I have in there on the curb and take his trash and put it in the trunk."

"Trash switching," I said. "Okay, you got it." I stepped out, and the ice crunching under my boots as I made the switch seemed as loud as gunshots. My heart was trip-hammering. I could feel the pulse in my throat and temples. Finally, I returned to the car, and snapped the door closed quietly.

Perryman slid the car on down the street like a ghost. "Whose trash was it that I left there?" I asked.

"Mine."

"How did you know what kind of trash bags he used?"

"They're probably not an exact match, but they're black."

"Black enough," I said.

"Now, we go through it," Perryman said.

"I know the drill."

"Yep. We need to examine everything."

"In your office?"

"I still have that generator, and it's powerful enough for a couple of rooms and we'll have our head lamps."

"This job sure isn't what I thought," I said.

"Tell me about it." The darkness must've made Perryman feel comfortably intimate because she said, "What got you into this work?"

"What got you into it?"

I saw Perryman's smile in the dash lights. "I asked you first."

I gusted a sigh and my hands twitched for my Zippo. "To tell you the truth, I'll need to smoke." I already had a Camel clamped between my lips.

Perryman shrugged and waited.

I rolled the window down, and the budding dreamy atmosphere was immediately swept away with the frigid wind that clutched at my throat.

"Well?" Perryman said angrily, glaring at the open window.

"It all started when Jesus was born."

"Give me a break."

"Okay, It started by being orphaned early on and deciding to dedicate my life to Christ."

Perryman took her eyes off the road to stare at me incredulously. She snorted.

"Watch it!" I jerked the wheel and we only clipped a trash cart but didn't knock it over. My sudden pull made the car swerve into a donut skid and Perryman panicked, stomping the brakes repeatedly and fighting the swerve by hauling the wheel to the left and cursing.

"We're stuck!" Perryman said. "Get out; fix it."

"You did this, you fix it. I'm fine right here. I saved you from having to pick up trash in the street like a convict."

"I'm driving, asshole. Push!"

I opened the door, stood up, threw my cigarette in the snow, and went to the hood and began pushing. The tires spun.

"Push! Keep pushing!"

"I'm not having a baby! You get out and push and I'll steer."

Perryman stood and slammed the door.

I smiled. "Just put your little delicate hands right here and I'll have us free in no time."

Perryman did as I told her, and I sat in the driver's seat and eased the car back and forth inch by inch, gaining traction millimeter by millimeter. Finally, we were out of the ruts and ready to go. I saw Perryman glance fearfully up the street as if Goodson might be watching; then she opened the driver's door and stood, tapping her boot until I got out.

Once we were back on the ice, slipping and sliding, she said, "So what happened?"

"You drive like a scared amateur and you freaked out. What do you think?"

"No," Perryman said, "what you were saying before."

I pointedly rolled down the window she had closed when I had been pushing and started a new cigarette. "Well, I saw that God was like the Wizard of Oz. Just a shit stain behind a curtain."

Perryman sucked her breath.

"And I decided to dedicate my life to doing something concretely good."

"No wonder," Perryman said softly.

"No wonder what?"

"You have this...tenderness. Under the surface, of course." Perryman glanced at me. "Way under," she added at my look.

"Bullshit."

"No, I've heard about it. Your chief told me. He's noticed that you can get suspects and wits to trust and confide in you. It's uncanny, he said, because you're as dumb as mud and a total mess, but you solve cases."

"Chief said that?" My face burned.

"That's why I requested we work together. I wanted to see for myself."

"And have you?" I said through my teeth.

"A little with that kid you brought with you the other day."

"Oh, fuckle, everyone likes kids. That's nothing, so don't think you're gathering evidence, Perryman."

"No, it's something else. Something more. You were connected. He was hooked into you and would've done anything you asked."

I flipped my Zip maniacally. I repeated the phrase I always said to deflect probing. "I'm just lucky."

Perryman laughed. We hit a speed bump of ice, and my head would've slammed against the window if it had been closed.

"That ain't luck," she said.

I lit another cigarette. "Suit yourself."

"So you skipped over a bunch."

"What?"

"You're not a cheerleader for Jesus one day and a homicide detective the next. What happened?"

"Sheriff, *please.*"

"Look, we've got a long drive out of these suburbs and we're working together. Lie to me."

I grinned. "That I can do." I threw my butt out the window and closed it. "I had this girlfriend at college and her father was an old timer homicide cop. He had seen it all, man. And he was tough as leather and twice as hard as steel. She brought me home one holiday and he didn't care for us dating. Like I said, he was real old school. He had married his high school sweetheart and she was a housewife with heels and pearls and the whole nine. But he wasn't a jerk about his daughter and me being a couple either, which made me respect him. Because where we were going to school claimed to put Jesus and His principles first, but hated and abused gays with a ferocity that still upsets me."

Perryman nodded.

I kept flipping my Zippo. I could smell the lighter fluid. "So if someone like that could earn my respect, maybe God is nonsense. Maybe this detective had something. It opened my eyes to a larger, saner world."

"Murder sane?"

"Well, compared to Christians."

Perryman choked and laughed.

"So he and I started talking. I saw that he was helping the world in a real way. I began to admire him. My curiosity grew, and he told me he saw something in me. A hunger." I smiled at the memory, studying my lap.

"A hunger, huh?" Perryman said.

"So anyway, I let go of all the fairy tales and got my degree and grabbed with both hands the chance to work with him. The homicide department was much smaller then, and he had a lot of pull and wanted to mentor me. His daughter and I had split up amicably long ago, and she went to Middlebury vet school and married a man. Another vet, I think."

"What was his name?"

"The husband?"

"*No,* your mentor."

"Kendall."

Perryman slowly turned to face me, the shock plain. "Kendall? He's a legend! He mentored you?"

I nodded, my throat thick.

"Jesus, no wonder you can do no wrong."

I let that go. "When he died, I…well, I had a meltdown."

"You had a mental break?"

"I just couldn't make it right. I couldn't recover, heal, move on, or work. I was paralyzed. So my chief sent me to South Dakota to try to get myself together." I snapped my lighter closed with finality and said brightly, "And here I am, all better!"

Perryman nodded. "I remember his funeral. Biggest one Tulsa had ever seen. They had to have three services to accommodate everyone. That preacher earned his money."

I blinked water out of my eyes. "He taught me everything I know. He taught me to carry VapoRub and cram it into my nostrils at decomps. He taught me how to interrogate. And that there's no such thing as good, old-fashioned police work; there's just police work. He told me everything…" I drifted on memories.

"Except?"

"Except how to deal with the nightmares and the insomnia."

"But you're okay?"

I shrugged. "Okay is as okay does. I'm here."

CHAPTER THIRTEEN

I emerged from the bathroom after brushing my teeth. I had been here five days. Since the whole house was cold and dark, we were living in just one room: the one with the fireplace. I saw Sophie sitting on the couch with the lit end of a flashlight in her mouth and her cheeks ballooned with air. She was looking at herself in a hand mirror. Her cheeks were glowing bright orange like a puffed-up blowfish.

"What are you doing?" I said.

Sophie collapsed against the couch as if her whole body were deflated. "I am so *bored!*"

It was then that I noticed the nearly empty wine glass. "Sophie, honey, do you realize how early it is?"

Sophie held the glass to the pale, thin, morning light, squinting at it and then tipped the last few drops into her mouth. "So? You got a problem, Rogers?"

I raised my hands. "No, ma'am. Where's Alistair?"

"He found a Laundromat with power and he is washing our clothes. Isn't he a prince?" Sophie sneered.

"That is very nice," I paused, "isn't it?"

"I am stir-crazy! He didn't want me to go so I wouldn't be stressed by the crowds or the work or endangered by traffic conditions." Sophie picked up her wine glass again. "Therefore, I am drunk."

"Well," I looked around the wreckage of the room. Three bodies in a confined space without heat or electricity produced a lot of litter. "We could pick up a little around here." I began gathering empty chip bags, Guinness bottles, pizza boxes, and candy wrappers. "Want me to restart the fire?"

"Who cares?" Sophie heaved herself upright, poured a fresh glass of wine, and handed me the empty bottle.

I went to the kitchen and dropped the bottles into recycling and stuffed the rest into the overflowing trash. "If you're so bored, you could take out your trash!" I called.

"Eat me!" Sophie said.

I returned to the living room. I turned on the gas jets, opened the flue, and lit the fireplace with my Zippo. I lit all the candles. I folded blankets and piled them together. I fluffed and replaced pillows. I gathered books and magazines into two tall stacks. I opened the curtains. Still no sun, but no more ice for the time being. I turned the battery-powered radio on to easy listening. I knelt in front of Sophie. "Baby, you've got to get yourself together."

Sophie set fire to my head with her flat stare. She gulped her glass of wine and slammed the empty stem onto the side table and slumped again.

"Don't let yourself unravel," I said.

Sophie snorted. "What do you care?" She stretched one leg and rested it on my shoulder, stretched the other, and placed it on top of the bottom leg, crossed at the ankles.

"Oh, I care!" I seethed.

Sophie rolled her eyes. "Yeah? How much?" She lifted the top leg, and with a twist of the foot of the bottom leg, hooked the back of my neck and pulled me forward. I stood up suddenly, throwing her legs to the side.

"Thought so," Sophie laughed, closing her eyes. I clenched my fists and counted silently. Sophie, her eyes still closed, sleepily said, "I've walked; I've read; I've napped; I've played board games and cards; I've eaten till I can't fit my pants," Sophie snapped her waistband, "and there's still no electricity!"

"Have you showered?"

Sophie's eyes opened slowly like a vampire's, mean and hungry. "I got your shower right here," she said, cupping her crotch.

"That's sweet," I said. "I'm gonna get a bath started for you."

"Mmf," Sophie said, wiggling her wine glass for a refill. "Mm starving."

I left her there splayed out like a wilted flower. I went through her clothes and found a sweater and jeans. Then I took a deep breath and dug through her panties drawer and pulled out underwear, socks, and a bra. I found one last thick clean bath towel that Alistair hadn't taken to launder, and I started the shower so it would be as hot as possible. I went to find Sophie.

She was in the kitchen, weaving at the counter, drunkenly sipping cold chicken noodle soup from the can, the jagged edge of the lid looking as if it would cut. "Sophie! Stop that!" I rushed to her side and took the soup. Blood was trickling down her mouth and chin from the laceration between her upper lip and nose. There was a film of blood floating on the top of the soup. I grabbed some paper towels, soaked them in cold water, and cleaned her up and held them to her injury. "Oh, baby, what have you done?" I murmured.

"Was hungry." Sophie whined.

"I'll feed you after your shower, okay? Come on." I led her to the bathroom, pushed her in, and shut the door behind her. Stripping and soaping her was beyond me. With my next breath, I involuntarily imagined Sophie in the shower. Oh, God. I leaned against the wall and slumped to the floor. Sophie, her eyes closed, steam rising, tendrils of lather snaking down down down her slick, silken skin, finding the quickest way over her curves from her delectable throat, tender and delicious as plump scallops, suds white and foamy, then easing lower to her breasts—pale and sweet as whipped cream, tipped with aching tart raspberries of delicate pink. The soap gathering in a slippery sheen, coating each breast in a clean, rainbow shellac and then sliding into the truffle cleft of her buttocks and the dripping lather of her ruby red pomegranate cunt and all the suds meeting there, the bubbles mingling and mixing, all the hot wetness so soft, before sliding gently down the smooth, carved alabaster that was her legs.

All that precious soap being wasted and washed down the drain. All those suds that knew Sophie in a way I didn't. All that lather that got to touch her and probe her crevices and ride down her spine and lick between her toes. That bar of soap that rubbed against her breasts, jiggling and lubricating them, readying them for me to consume Sophie completely and leave only a husk. That bar of soap that tickled her golden red pubic hair, filling the folds with lather, combining her pineapple slickness with soap suds, Sophie's fingers slowly parting and opening her secrets, washing her fantasies down the drain.

Was she under the hot spray of water, hoping I would come in? Was she sitting on the floor of the shower, her legs open, her fingers trying to imitate me, her mind sending me scorching messages of desire, wishing I would walk in and take her? Was she imagining me just on the other side of this door, in torment? Was that making her bath sweeter?

"Fuck that," I said, standing up in a surge. I flung open the bathroom door, and on my way to the huge glass shower cube that was opaque with steam, I tore off my clothes and dropped them in the path of my charge. I jerked open the shower door and walked in, temporarily blinded by vapor clouds.

I was going to eat her alive. Sophie would have no say except yes. I would bend her backward and she would drip and melt like crystal sugar into honey. Her breasts would be turgid with lust, and I would ravish them, marking her once and for all forever. I would bite my way down her ribs and lift her into the air, pressing her back against the marble shower wall and raising her cunt to face level where at last, *finally,* I would take Sophie's vibrating pearl into my mouth, and we would be joined.

Sophie's screams would demolish the house around us, but still I would pleasure her, the ground zero of her orgasms rippling through me like little earthquakes. I would be her succubus and she my everlasting food. When she cried no more, I would plunge my arm in her trembling cunt up to my elbow and impale her on my hard, brown arm. I would only stop once all thoughts of Sophie had been obliterated and not even a flutter of desire remained for either of us. Then I would gently fold Sophie into me and we would sleep where we lay.

The hot shower, with its multiple heads and hard spray, was very soothing as I felt my way into it. The stall was the size of a steam room, so Sophie could be anywhere. I stretched out my arms, expecting a delighted shriek any second. I touched the wall. Empty! I snapped off the water, and the steam cleared and the chill set in immediately. The silence was eerie. I stepped out of the shower, grabbing the towel. Sophie was fully dressed and curled up like a fist by the spa tub. She was sleeping and snoring softly. My desire evaporated like the steam. As my skin cooled, I got goose flesh, and I could feel my jawbone tensing as if my teeth were about to start chattering. "Shit," I whispered, scrubbing myself dry, getting dressed, and standing in front of the fire until I was warm. I left Sophie on the floor to wake up on her own.

CHAPTER FOURTEEN

R ogers? Have you just quit working? Why aren't you in the office? Have you solved all the crimes? What the hell are you up to?" I had answered the phone after having woken from a fireside nap, and I was now chewing on a cold slice of pizza like a cow with cud. I rubbed my eyes.

"Who is this?" I asked sleepily. I knew exactly who it was: Perryman. But she needed tweaking. I swallowed and then finished a leftover glass of red wine that was sitting on the coffee table.

"Goddamn you, it's the sheriff! Have you been fired or something?"

"Honey, slow down. I have not been fired. Homicide is on winter hiatus." I reached for another stiff slice of pizza. "In case you haven't heard, we're right at the epicenter of a natural disaster."

The latest news was that two million people were without power and that there was no end in sight. The power company had three shifts working around the clock, and electric workers from all over the nation were converging on Tulsa to help. There were trucks here from Texas, Missouri, Illinois, New Mexico, and North Carolina. Restoring power was at a snail's pace because of all the trees. The urban forest was old and extensive.

All those trees were experiencing an arboreal holocaust and were dropping limbs, splitting in two all the way to the roots, or keeling over whole, blocking traffic and exposing their enormous root balls. Cars were crushed, houses were cleaved, roads closed, and power lines snatched from poles as the trees went down as if they were thrashing and flailing for lifelines; their bodies so overloaded with ice they gave out, unable to support all that weight for one more second. Sub-stations were pummeled into exploding darkness. It was like living during the time of dinosaurs, and extinction was causing them to drop dead where they stood. And this city was lousy with dinosaurs. Tulsa prided itself on what a green, forested cityscape it had, and now that was crashing down like bombs of ice while we helpless humans cowered in the cold blackness.

"That's no excuse!" Perryman said. "While you've been eating bonbons, I've been solving this case! We found his girlfriend!"

"Smooth," I said. "What about the financials?"

"On the way. I'm telling you, after this, Jesus Jim will have to prosecute!"

"Careful," I said. "Don't get your hopes up. So you need me for something?" I picked ham off the rest of the pizza.

"Just to remind you that you have a job to do."

I rolled my eyes and stared out the window just as a great limb snapped off and fell to the ground with a boom and shatter. "Perryman, honey, you're a bore." I ended the call and my phone rang again immediately. "Rogers," I sighed.

"I need help starting a fire. I'm all cold and stuff."

"Well, hello, Penelope." I licked my lips.

CHAPTER FIFTEEN

The next day, I woke up tangled in sheets. The roar of the generator outside and the portable heater in the room reminded me that I was in Penelope's bed.

After Penelope's phone call, I waited on the curb for her to pick me up. She never said a word to me after, "nice to meet you," when I got in her car. She lived in a small bungalow not far from Sophie. Once at her house, I walked around in amazement, flicking on lights, opening the refrigerator, and even turning on the television. After so many days with shadows and nights with candles, Penelope's house seemed bright and loud to the point of garishness. I felt like a caveman, goggling at the portable heaters and Penelope's glowing computer screen.

"How?" I asked, staring at the sparkling chandelier over her dining table. Penelope pointed out the window where there was a great box like a jet engine and sounding as loud as if we had parked on the runway.

"Right." I nodded and turned back to Penelope who handed me a glass of champagne and then took off her blouse as I sipped the drink. I didn't care about power anymore; I lost myself in her doe-brown eyes, small, tight afro, nutmeg skin, and supple body. Penelope wasn't wearing a bra, and her breasts were so high and tight, they looked cast in bronze. Her nipples were tantalizing thimbles of chocolate. As Penelope removed her wool slacks, my mind reeled. I've met eager, but this was new. She left her high-heeled leather boots on. I gulped the wine. Penelope strode naked to the refrigerator, removed the champagne bottle, and refilled my glass. Then she sipped from my flute, drew my lips to hers, and let the liquid trickle into my mouth.

Penelope led me to her bedroom and I was astonished at the warmth. Penelope could be naked and not cold. I could see where I was going without a flashlight or candle. Sophie's house seemed so dark, chilled, and antiquated, like a castle in Dickensian times.

Penelope threw me on the bed and landed on top of me, ripping away my clothes. I was helpless as she jerked my jeans off. I tried to hold her, but she was like a wild animal, fierce, silent, and unstoppable. She kissed my neck and clawed at my skin. I clamped my mouth on one nipple and tugged. She yelped and smacked me, but I knew she liked it and wanted more. I seized the other nipple and bit. She groaned and dug her nails into my back. I heard her panting so I spread her cunt and caressed her slick clit and shoved three fingers in deep.

Penelope clutched my throat in a vise grip and my eyes bulged. I grabbed her waist to draw her closer and I fucked her harder. When I began to see stars from lack of oxygen, I pulled my hand out, and Penelope slapped me. I tasted blood from the inside of my cheek. I swatted her ass. Penelope smiled and leaned over me, opened a drawer, and withdrew a thick, black dildo. She strapped me in and straddled the dildo. I tried to help or to touch her, but Penelope kept hitting me until I was subdued. I watched hungrily as she slid down the cock, enveloping its entire shaft. She rode the cock, her buttocks slapping my thighs, her eyes closed, her taut breasts barely bouncing.

She let me brush her turgid clit occasionally with my thumb. I flicked it and she moaned. Penelope worked that dick, changing rhythms, riding fast, faster. Finally, I began caressing her clit continuously, and Penelope stopped altogether and arched back, pushing her pussy forward for me. I cupped one buttock and stroked her fast. Penelope came with an eagle scream and began gyrating on the dildo so hard, I knew I'd be bruised. When she calmed, instead of smiling, crying, or crawling into my arms, Penelope leaned over me again and handed me lube and a butt plug. Then, without raising her cunt off the dildo, she turned around and put her ass in my face and began riding the dildo slowly, her hands braced on my thighs.

I tickled her asshole, wishing I could eat it up. Instead, I squirted lube on to the plug and eased it into her anus. Penelope shuddered and curled, moving so slowly. I savored every second of that sight: the black, shiny dildo, the juicy pussy, the hard, round ass, and the black rosebud anus. I gently fucked her with the plug as she rode my cock.

Penelope leaned all the way back toward me, relaxing to let herself be filled completely. She reached for my hand and pulled it around to touch her clit, and I stroked her gently and got harder and faster as I followed her lead. She had a deep orgasm marked only by a grunt and sweat droplets landing on my belly.

Penelope pulled out the plug and eased herself off me. I opened my arms to receive her and she scowled. She lay on her back next to me and opened her legs wide enough to split in two. She began slipping her fingers inside until I stood up. I pulled her to the edge of the bed and teased her cunt with the cock. She whined and gyrated. I started to plunge in, but she closed her knees. She placed her pussy-wet finger on my lips. I nodded and rummaged in her bedside table drawer for a dam. All she had was a roll of Saran so I wrapped her and began licking and sucking. And so it went, all night.

When I woke, I still had the dildo strapped on me and Penelope was gone.

Penelope's bedroom was blindingly bright with morning sun. I heard ice sliding off trees and roofs and crashing to the ground. The generator must have run out of gas.

I stood up slowly, stepped out of the strap-on, and limped to the bathroom. I was just assessing myself in the mirror when Penelope appeared, perfectly groomed and dressed in a silk skirt and cashmere twinset. She threw my clothes at me and said, "Come on, stud. Let's go."

She began to turn away then approached again. "God, you have a fine ass for a jasper." She bent and chomped me hard on one buttock.

I jerked away. "That's enough. Just let me dress." I held out the harness and dildo. "You can put this in the dishwasher now."

Penelope took it and unnerved me by watching as I put all my clothes back on. It took a while because I had been layered against the cold.

She never said another word until she pulled her car to a stop in front of Sophie's. "It was fun. I'll call you." She reached across me and opened my door.

I got out, my spine popping, my legs aching a little. Before I could turn to say good-bye, Penelope sped away, slipping on the ice that was still too thick to have melted.

I stood, blinking in the sunshine like a lost mole. I clicked my lighter and did a few finger passes. I walked up the stairs and noticed Sophie bundled in a parka and wearing sunglasses and holding binoculars, sitting on the top step.

"What are you doing?" I asked.

Sophie jerked the binoculars to her face and studied something in the distance with great concentration. I turned to look at whatever she was watching. "Power trucks," Sophie said. "I've seen them all over the neighborhood. They've got to be getting close."

I laughed. "Getting a little impatient?"

Sophie raised the binocs to look at my face, flinched, and lowered them. "Are those hickies? You nasty dog."

"What? Uh, no. Just bruises from…work." I raised my collar.

"That is so tacky," Sophie said and raised the binoculars again to stare down the street. "I saw one! I saw it!"

"Hey, my cell needs to be charged, can I plug it into your car?"

"Mine's out there now, but you can after mine is finished." Sophie answered faintly, still gazing at the horizon.

My phone rang. "Rogers, hurry, my phone is going dead."

"You tiger," Marny purred. "I knew you would like her."

"Like her? I've never met her."

"What? Penelope told me—"

"She spoke to you? Because she never said a word to me, just put my money on the dresser."

"Ooo, that's a very good sign."

"She never even kissed me!" I said.

"Am I sensing dissatisfaction? Of all people—"

"No," I said, watching Sophie. "No, I just think I was had."

Marny's laugh gurgled. "Of course you were, darling. I told her you were pure sex on legs. That she should eat you on a cracker and forget the cracker." Marny laughed again. "So, you're welcome. You owe me, darling."

"I owe you a slap. I was two hundred pounds of chum!"

Marny giggled. "Don't you *love* that feeling? You're welcome," she repeated.

"You're welcome to kiss my Injun ass."

"You know I only experimented in college and that was for a luscious sable coat. So I'm calling because there's a new case."

"Tell me." I sat next to Sophie in the sun.

"I see it!" Sophie yelled, dropping the binoculars onto the frozen grass and taking off at a careful trot, her booted feet thumping on the ice as I saw a big white truck lumber around the corner.

"The entire city is shut down; I can't get any motherfucking tobacco, but people can still kill each other." I checked my pouch for cigarettes: only twelve left. I put a Camel in my mouth, rolled my Zippo in a finger pass up and down, up and down, finally, lighting my cigarette and puffing contentedly into the warmth of the sunshine, enjoying listening to the ice drop like slushy stones into the melt. The ice that had held the city in its clear, slick prison, hard as diamonds, heavy as gravity, dangerous as poison, was finally loosening its death grip and sliding away, drop by drop, chunk by chunk, leaving us to clean up.

"Be that as it may, Socrates, there's a couple you need to talk to before you go to the scene."

"Yeah?"

"Southside Willie and L Bow."

"Not the gruesome twosome."

"Oh, darling, do you like your job or not?"

"What is this?"

"All right, here's where to go."

My phone went dead. "Damn!"

Sophie came around the corner, looking dejected. She dropped down next to me with a sigh. "Gimme one." She took a cigarette, put it in her mouth, and leaned close to touch her cigarette to mine. For a few dazzling seconds, our faces were so close. But then I worried she could smell last night on me so I pulled back. Sophie inhaled and closed her eyes. "So here's the deal. They won't get to us today. They are repairing grids by size priority. The grids that serve the largest number of people get fixed first. And this," Sophie gestured to Maple Park, "is one of the smallest grids in town. Who knew? Who thinks of that when buying a house?"

"So any ETA?"

Sophie laughed bitterly. "Couple of days doubtful, next week definitely."

"*Next week?*" I yelled.

"Yeah." Sophie shrugged. "But at least we have water, right?" She shook her head, smoking thoughtfully.

"Next week, I can't do that. I just can't do it. I can't," I babbled. "I'll go stay in a hotel or I'll check myself into the hospital. I just can't do it."

Sophie stared at me. "What is the matter with you? Why are you so upset?"

"I—" the words froze in my throat and I didn't say, "because I'm in love with you and it's torture to stay here, but I can't go home." The thought of being in love was so new to me that I shut my mouth and stared stubbornly at the skyline.

"Hey, the courthouse has power, so you can at least go to your office, right?" Sophie said.

I turned on her. "My office is at *city hall*, not the goddamned courthouse, okay? If you want me to leave, just say so!" I was panting and I stared at Sophie, wanting to hate her. This was all her fault. Sophie raised her eyebrows and exterminated the cigarette with a small hiss in a puddle on the sidewalk. I would love to kiss her now. To taste my tobacco in her mouth.

She said, "Stay, go, courthouse, city hall, Jimmy crack corn and I don't care." She stood and returned to the house.

"Jimmy crack corn and she don't care," I said to myself as I plugged my phone into Sophie's car to recharge. "I'll be goddamned."

Chapter Sixteen

I turned when I heard a car horn. It was Perryman leaning out to yell at me, "Come on! We have him in custody!"

As I walked down the drive to join Perryman, I noticed Sophie watching me quizzically as she swept slush off the front steps. "I'll be home for dinner, honey!" I said.

"Bite me," Sophie said. "Why don't you bring dinner for once?"

I blew a kiss and slammed Perryman's car door.

"Your wife?" Perryman said sourly.

"I'm touched! You do care. Don't be upset. There's plenty of me to go around." I slid the seat all the way back, propped my feet on the dash, and lit a cigarette.

Perryman stopped the car, swatted my boots, pinched my cigarette, and flicked it out the window, and thumped her index finger on the scab on my forehead. "Put your feet down, no smoking, and shut up, you immature savage."

"You are such a rag."

"Detective Rogers, remember yourself."

I had nothing to say to that so we rode in silence. I played with my Zippo. "This slush," Perryman finally said, holding the steering wheel steadily against the bucking car, "is more treacherous," Perryman grunted, braking and turning away from a mogul, "than solid ice."

"And so close to Christmas too." I mused, bracing myself as the car jolted.

"What does that mean?"

"Nothing," I said with a smile.

We parked at the county jail. The long, low building was lurid with lights against the darkening skyline. I could see another gray cloud bank fattening and building in the north, gradually obliterating the deep, clear blue sky.

"This place was relying on a huge supply of emergency generators for a few days. Then PSO got them back on the grid," Perryman said as we crunched and splashed toward the door.

I thought of Sophie's dark, silent home and my own stone-cold house abandoned all these days. Perryman signed us in and we went to an interrogation room and waited.

"Here are his new charges." Perryman handed me a booking sheet.

"Phew!" I said. "Resisting arrest, obstructing, assault and battery on a police officer, defrauding an innkeeper, throwing human waste on police officer. Defrauding an innkeeper?"

"Found him holed up in a Motel 6. They tipped us."

There was a rattling of chains and unlocking of doors, and Rick Goodson shuffled in and sat at the table.

"You want him locked to the wall, Sheriff?"

"No, thank you. We'll be fine."

The door locked behind the deputy and we were alone with the suspect. He looked haggard and had a black eye.

"Well, well, well, Ricky, what do you have to say for yourself?" I slid the booking sheet toward him. "This was quite a scene. Was it your honeymoon?"

Goodson said nothing.

"This will go so much better for you if you cooperate. You're just making the inevitable also painful. Don't I always say that, Dana? I always say it's better to cooperate."

"Every single day," Perryman said.

Goodson was silent.

"Come on, Ricky. Tell us what really happened. You'll feel better," I said.

"I don't know how you fabricated this case against me, but it will never stick. I didn't do this, and when I get out, I'll sue you into hell," Rick said through gritted teeth.

"Well, I've got something to show you." Perryman removed from her briefcase two clear evidence bags. One contained small snow boots and the other, large rubber shoe soles. "Mind explaining that?"

Goodson shrugged. "A bag of trash?"

"Precisely! Glad you mentioned that." Perryman produced one last bag containing large snow boots with the soles cut off. The edges of the boots were ragged where a serrated knife had sloppily sawed.

"You got a rabbit in there too?" I asked.

"If it would help convict this son of a bitch, I sure would." Perryman grinned.

"Hey, wait a minute!" Goodson cried. "You're gonna try to railroad me into prison! Well, fuck you; I'm innocent."

"Then why are you still sitting here, my friend?" I asked. "Why don't you demand your lawyer, clam up, and go back to your cell?" I stroked the table as if it were Sophie's thigh. Goodson licked his lips. "I'll tell you why. Because you're guilty and you want to know what we have on you. How good our case is." I stared him down until he dropped his eyes then I whispered, "Our case is solid. How good is your attorney?"

"Your evidence is *that?*" Goodson sneered at the shoes.

"Yep," Perryman said. "You thought everything through. You were really smart. Gotta give you props for smart."

A smile twitched on to Goodson's face for a split second.

"You have small feet and you knew we'd check footprints at the scene, so you bought these boots," Perryman held up the bag with the mutilated boot tops, "and you cut off the soles. Then, see this?" Perryman pointed to the large, rubber soles in another bag. "You glued the bottoms to your own shoes. See here? These fit together nicely and they both have glue residue on them. Now, when you deliberately tromped through the scene, you'd mislead us into looking for a huge man. Very smart."

These were the moments I lived for. To sift through garbage and get to nail a piece of trash.

Sweat had popped out on Goodson's upper lip. He furtively swiped at it and then tried to laugh. "That's it? You gotta be kidding me."

"Capital murder, son," I said. I clicked open my Zippo, struck a flame, and did a graceful, rolling finger pass.

"How do you not get burned?" Perryman asked me.

"Because I know better," I said, staring at Goodson.

"I need to call the DA." Goodson stood and pounded on the door. When the guard opened it, Goodson barked, "Get Jim Harrison on the phone." The guard said nothing and closed the door and re-locked it.

"Jesus Jimmy being your friend isn't going to help you now," I said.

"Why were you staying at the Motel 6?" Perryman asked.

"None of your goddamn business!" Goodson said.

"You're wrong there. Now that you're being charged with murder, everything in your whole life is ours. If we need to know what you got for Christmas when you were six, we'll interrogate your mother. You've forfeited any claim on your life," I said.

"What about innocent until proven guilty?" Goodson said.

"That twaddle is for the courts. It's just the three of us and we all know what happened," I said. I heard Alistair say "twaddle" and "rubbish," and I liked them both and had begun using them.

"I know about Jessica," Perryman said hoarsely. Goodson jerked as if he had been touched with an electric wire, and he glared at the sheriff with eyes blazing. "And that your marriage was over."

"What?" Goodson stalled.

"We also know about the debt," I said.

"The what? You're not making any sense."

"And I have your cell records," Perryman added.

"You what?"

"We also have your computer, but there's no reason for us to get a forensic analyst into all that is there? If you help us, we'll help you," I bluffed.

The silence that followed was like a sound vacuum. None of us moved. Finally, Goodson stood and said, "I did not do this. I am finished cooperating."

"Funny, you haven't even started," I said.

"That's fine, sir. Thank you for talking to us. Here's my card," Perryman tried to hand it to Goodson, who let it drop to the floor. "Just call me if you change your mind." Perryman pounded on the door and the guard let all of us out.

On the way to Perryman's car, I capered around her like a puppy. "Slam dunk, Perryman!"

She smiled, her entire face glowing. "Thank you," then more to herself, "I *will* make something good out of that sow's ear office. Just watch me."

When she dropped me off at Sophie's, she said, "See you in court!"

When I opened the front door, I smelled pizza. "Not again," I groaned.

Sophie appeared with a bottle of red wine. "Is there a woman on earth you won't fuck, Rogers?"

I grinned. "Just one."

"I got your cell out of my car, and it has been ringing nonstop. Take care of it, will you?" Sophie viciously yanked the cork from the wine bottle and went to the living room.

I followed her and knelt before the dark fireplace and lit it. "Where's Alistair?"

"Don't worry. He's here." Sophie paused, sighing voluptuously. "He's in the shower."

Before I could slap her, my phone rang. "I better take this," I snapped.

"Step outside with your dirt. I don't want to hear it," Sophie said.

"Fuck you," I told Sophie, who smiled. She had never looked more appetizing. I took the call on the front porch.

"Have you ever been to Tijuana?" the voice asked.

"Penelope! Hello, baby, what you know good?"

"You free tonight?" She giggled. The lighthearted laugh disguised her ground-zero-style seduction.

I thought quickly. My back was still in spasm from our last evening together. "Oh, I'm sorry, honey pot. I'm busy with the man tonight."

"What's he got you doing?" Penelope moaned with longing. My clit twitched, trying to change my mind.

"Oh, you know, stompin' devils."

"I hear that. Well, may the Lord bless you or the mortuary will dress you. I'll call another time." She hung up. I suspected she was already dialing someone else. Before I could return inside, my phone rang.

"You curbin' me?" Marny asked.

"No, phone's been dead."

"You don't have power yet?"

"No, do you?"

"Of course, silly. And it is *wonderful.* I'm running the television, computer, vacuum, dishwasher, microwave, and of course, I have the heat up as high as it will go. How are you?"

"Fine. What about that other murder?"

"No worries. They sent Holmes out."

"Holmes! I am sitting on my thumb with nothing to do and no power and you call Holmes?"

"Oh, dear, what a bore."

"Where is it?"

"I left my files at the office. Are you ever going to report to the chief by the way?"

"Don't change the subject."

"From what, work to work?"

"Where's the scene?"

Marny sighed. "You need a wife."

"Where's the scene, Claw?"

Marny sucked air. "That's low. You said you'd never call me that again."

"Emergency measures, what can I tell you?"

Claw was short for Claw Mark, which I nicked her after Marny fell for a married man, and in my heartfelt attempt to talk her out of the affair, I told her that she would only be a claw mark on the guy's back, nothing more, which is exactly what happened.

"I hate you."

"I know, baby. Where's the scene?"

"I don't remember."

"Like hell. What are you doing to me?"

"Something wicked this way comes and you're in the middle of the road."

"What?" I scratched my head.

"One word: Goodson."

"Make sense."

"Watch the news. I'm not saying."

"Spill, heifer."

"You're lucky I told you this much."

I punched my phone dead and heard an ominous creak. When I looked up to see if a tree limb was going to impale me, a load of slush pounded me to the ground.

"Goddammit!" I yelled. "Fuck this motherfucking job, this motherfucking town, this motherfucking ice storm, and this motherfucking blackout!"

Sophie opened the door and smothered a laugh when she saw me crumpled on the ground. "Do you mind?" she asked haughtily. "The baby is sleeping! And this is a family show."

I stood up shakily, brushing ice from my clothes. "Fuck you twice."

"You had the chance."

I debated about grabbing her or telling her off, but instead just said tiredly. "I know. I blew it."

Sophie's face softened and she looped her arm through mine. "Come on. I'll make some soup and a bourbon for you."

"Sounds great. Forget the soup."

CHAPTER SEVENTEEN

I was nursing my second bourbon that Sophie had simmered hot on the gas stove when my phone rang. I was wearing sweats, holding my steaming mug, sitting in front of the fire, wrapped in a comforter.

"Yeah?" I said sleepily.

"Rogers! What the fuck are you up to?"

The DA. I sat up, the comforter falling away. I took a gulp of my hot bourbon, sweet fire licking flames from my belly to my brain. "Could you be more specific?"

"You and Perryman better come to my office ASAP."

"Jimbo, at the moment, I am not available."

"*Not available?* You better come see me this afternoon or I'll have your badges."

I stood up, forgetting the chill. "On what grounds?" I said, but the phone was already dead. "That sorry shack of sit," I slurred.

"What's up?" Sophie sat across from me, a steaming mug of hot chocolate in her hands.

"That's no substitute for me," I said, grinning goofily.

"Give it a rest, willya, Chief?" Sophie said. She gestured to my cell. "What's going on?"

"That no-balled bitch DA just pisses me off."

Sophie drank from her mug, her eyes closed in delight. She licked the chocolate moustache from her lip. The cut under her nose was healing well. "Mmm, better to be pissed off than pissed on."

Sophie's remark tickled me unexpectedly, and I cackled then as if a cork had been popped. Laughter burst out of me. It burbled and barked, circling and rising, leaving me breathless and Sophie wide-eyed. "Are you happy?" I asked, suddenly serious.

"Are you?"

"Hell, no. I'm too smart to be happy."

"Or too stupid," Sophie said meaningfully.

That sent me into a snorting fit of laughter again. Sophie cautiously moved my bourbon out of reach, which made me laugh more. My cell rang.

"Rogers." I hiccupped.

"Are you going to see the DA?" Perryman said.

"No way in hell. It's icy, the office is closed, and I'm full of firewater."

"Big Chief, you are a degenerate."

"Perryman, you're a drip. I don't have to ask if you're going in."

"I'm not."

I sucked air. Sophie finished her cocoa and went to the kitchen. "But he said he would have our badges," I said, impressed.

"On what grounds?" Perryman said.

"That's what I said!" I crowed, retrieving my bourbon and wrapping myself in blankets again. Suddenly, I wished Perryman liked me. "Say, you want to head over here for a drink?" I sipped mine and smacked my lips.

"Have you lost your mind? Is that all you think about?"

I watched Sophie as she returned and curled up by the fire with a croissant. "No, I think about one other thing," I said.

Perryman groaned. "You nauseate me."

"That's right before the baby in the baby carriage, right?"

"Over and out."

Sophie offered me half her croissant. "I don't want that girly food," I said.

"Only you would be such a pig to make food sexist."

I grinned. "I think you look real sexist in those jeans."

Sophie shook her head, her eyes flat. Alistair entered. "Sophie, I found an open Chinese take away on Seventy-first Street. Is that far?"

"God love the Orientals!" I said, my stomach roaring.

"It might take a while, but we can get there." Sophie stood, brushing off crumbs. "Can you be trusted not to have an orgy or burn down the house?"

"Absolutely not," I said.

"Cheeky bugger!" Alistair laughed.

"Maybe I should stay and guard the bar...the silver...the matches...the bedroom," Sophie said.

"No, you're coming. I don't know where to go. Jill, mate, keep your nose clean, all right?"

My mouth twitched. "Nose? Sure."

"Lovely, let's go." Alistair held out his hand. "Get a wiggle on, Soph." With a final worried glance, Sophie let him lead her out of the house.

My phone rang. "Marny! Tell me something good!"

"I'm fighting crime with my twat."

"Of course you are. The most powerful pudendum in Gotham City. How are you doing it this time?"

"Just flipping through these crime scene photos. You never see a good mani-bush on a vic. Have you ever noticed that?"

I scratched the scab on my forehead. "Now that you mention it, you're right."

"That's what I'm saying! By regular waxing, I'm ensuring that I'm not a victim. Ergo, grooming equals safety. I'm stopping crime with my Brazilian."

I snorted. "Good for you, McGruff."

"Meet me on the street in ten."

"I'm at a..." my voice caught, "friend's." I coughed. "Hazel Street."

"Got it. Be ready."

CHAPTER EIGHTEEN

While I waited for Marny on the stoop, I cursed the clouds that were gathering and thickening like dark blankets drawn over the scalding cold day. "Goddamn," I said, blowing on my hands. "More ice coming." As if to punctuate that statement, a tree down the street cracked in two and crashed to the ground, splitting the heavy silence like a cannon. I heard Marny's car bumping along the ice ruts long before I saw her. She was a clumsy driver even on dry roads. I went to the curb and she tried to stop, but her car kept sliding down the street.

"Help! Jill! Help!" I heard Marny shriek. I walked alongside the car as it slipped and bucked over the frozen street. Marny struggled, trying to turn the car and stomping the brakes. She lowered the passenger window. "Do something!" she yelled as I easily kept pace with the coasting car.

I laughed. "Yes, Master!" I put my finger on my nose and wiggled it.

"Goddamn your Native soul to hell!" Marny screeched.

"Way to convince me to help!" I said then carefully quickened my step until I was in front of the car. I walked backward as the car kept sliding forward. I took a deep breath, put my hands on the hood, and pushed against the car. I dug my boots into the pitted ice. The car pushed me forward several yards then stopped. "Now what?" I grunted.

"Just stay like that until the ice melts." Marny called from the driver's seat.

"This is the worst meeting I've ever been to!" The car's weight pushed me forward a few more feet. "You could've just sent a memo!" A cluster of branches crashed to the ground ten feet away, spraying us with ice chips.

"Get in!" Marny said.

"And do what? I'm not going to complete your Thelma and Louise fantasy for you, honey. I can't let go or your car will glide straight down that hill." I gestured with my head to the steep grade a block away. "If I could find a rock, we could try to block your momentum that way, but I don't see anything. We need to try to steer your car into an ice bank or up into someone's yard."

Marny's teeth were chattering. "What do I do?"

"What did I just say?" I said. "I'm going to move to the left and try to push your vehicle into that driveway on the right. You do what you can at the wheel to help. Ready?"

"No!" She said. I moved anyway and fell on the car's left front panel with fierce determination.

"Turn! Turn!" I yelled, shoving. My feet scrabbled as if I were on ball bearings.

"I'm trying!"

The car moved inexorably forward, carried on the smooth, slick grooves of ice, our meager human efforts yielding nothing. I groaned and pushed so hard I thought my bladder would burst. Instead, I fell flat on my belly, biting my tongue. The car cruised lazily on without me, just missing my outstretched hands.

"What now!" Marny screamed as the car gained speed.

"Either go down with it or abandon ship!" I said, swallowing blood.

The driver's door blew open, and Marny's expensively booted legs flailed in the air like a confused spider's.

"Jump and roll!" I said.

"This is Chanel!" Marny said.

I shrugged. "Die pretty!"

Marny flung herself onto the ice as the car crunched on. She rolled awkwardly, losing her hat and scarf. I walked to her, picking up her things. I helped her up, and we held on to each other as we followed the car to the crest of the hill.

"Beautiful," I said, chuckling, as the vehicle nose-dived down the steep street and gained speed.

Marny, white-faced and open-mouthed, watched. "Jesus, please help me. Please. If you do, I promise—" Marny's voice was cut off by the crash of her car into a downed tree at the bottom of the hill. "Crap on a cracker," she said.

"At least it didn't go into the river," I said brightly.

"Fuck off."

"Your daddy will buy you another Beemer."

Marny poisoned me with her stare.

"No one was hurt!" I added.

Marny jerked her hat and scarf out of my hand and retorted, "No thanks to *you*. And *look* at me!"

"Now hold on. You're the one who can't drive and decided it was an emergency to see me."

Marny's eyes blazed. "To *help* you!" She covered her face with her wadded scarf. I embraced her.

"Come on, settle down," I soothed her. "We will go back to Sophie's, call your insurance company, have a drink, and you can tell me everything." Marny nodded against my chest. As I started walking, I felt hard pellets peppering my scalp, lodging in the stiff brush of my hair. "More ice," I said.

Marny looked down the hill one last time at her totaled car. With a hiccupping sigh, she turned her back and walked away with me. "It's the end of the world," she said, her voice tiny and sad.

CHAPTER NINETEEN

So what's up?" I asked after I had wrapped Marny in a blanket in front of the fire and gave her a mug of tomato juice I had heated and improved with the liberal addition of Stoli. Marny's clothes were draped over the fireplace screen and steaming gently.

"Well." Marny took a long swallow. "This is putrid by the way."

"Oh no! Can I get you something else? A hot toddy with organic honey and freshly squeezed lemon juice and bee pollen? Perhaps a scone with Irish butter and homemade jam?" I flicked her on the head. "Talk."

"Your boy Goodson is a major contributor to Jim's campaign. There will be no filing. And you're looking good for getting fired for insubordination."

I sniffed. "Good luck to him. What else?"

"I was picking you up to go to a scene. Call just came."

"Robbery? Drugs?"

"Double homicide. Looks like a fire and two bodies."

"*What the fuck!*" I screeched, noting with embarrassment, my voice's resemblance to a howler monkey. I punched my phone. Goddamn these contraptions! I make two calls and it has to be recharged. "St. John! I'm still on the force, aren't I?" I said to the chief. "Then why am I being told about jobs I'm not on by sassy little ADAs with legs for days?"

Marny, who was sipping her drink, choked with laughter. She blushed, pleased, and curled into a tighter wool ball. "They couldn't reach you. They sent Honegger," she said.

"Uh huh, yes, I see. Got it." I smacked the phone down. "They couldn't reach me. They sent Honegger."

"You don't say?" Marny smiled dreamily. "This junk is gaining favor." She waggled her empty mug.

"Fuck that!" I said, adrenaline screaming through me like lightning bolts. I was dancing like a boxer. "We've gotta go!"

"You need to relax," Marny slurred. "Called Penelope lately?"

I leaned over Marny and breathed fire into her face. "*I. Said. Fuck. That.*" I ripped the blanket away from her body. "Let's go!"

Marny grabbed the blanket back. "Uncool, Jill." She swaddled herself into a cocoon. "Got a car?"

I stopped and slumped into a wingback chair. "Fuckle."

"We're back!" Alistair said. He and Sophie entered with their arms loaded with sacks. "Brilliant. More unexpected visitors," Alistair said and held out his hand to Marny. "Alistair Bellingham."

"Marny Marlowe. Enchanted." They shook hands.

Sophie looked at me, alarmed. "How do you two know each other?" Sophie said, her voice shrill. "I mean...are you two...er..."

"Bloody brilliant, Soph," Alistair laughed.

"No," Marny answered with a finality that closed all questions.

"Not yet," I said with a leer, "but soon." I crossed my fingers and held them in front of Sophie, who grimaced.

"Let's eat." Alistair sat next to Marny and began opening sacks and passing out egg rolls.

I swatted mine away. "I need your car," I said, standing expectantly and holding out my hand.

"Are you daft? It's fierce out there," Alistair said, crunching a wonton.

Sophie appraised me from head to foot. She made me feel dirty and unkempt. My scalp and neck itched like I needed a trim to my flattop, my eyes felt gummy, my breath sour, my body flaky and stale, my clothes mismatched, ill-fitting, and ripe. "No," she answered, her voice like liquid chocolate.

"Why?" I said. Alistair and Marny looked from Sophie to me and back as if they were following a tennis match. It was obvious this was deeper than the car.

"Because I need you where I can keep an eye on you. Whatever this is; it can wait until tomorrow when the weather and visibility might be better," Sophie said silkily, not meeting my blazing gaze.

"Fuck that!" I shouted. "We're not married! You don't own me!"

"But I do own my car." Sophie grinned and set a carton of fried rice in front of me. I kicked the rice, launching it into the air as if it were a confetti bomb. Rice rained down on the three of them and the carton landed several feet away and skittered on the wood floor.

"Then I'll call a taxi!" I yelled from the kitchen.

Sophie, who hadn't reacted to my fit, kept eating and answered, "Fine." Alistair and Marny wisely stayed silent. Marny picked rice out of Alistair's hair. I jab-dialed a taxi service. I got a recording that they were on skeleton staff and if I left a message, they would get back to me as soon as they could. "Goddammit!" I hated being in the kitchen away from the fire. It was cold. I turned up all four gas burners on the stove and lit them with my Zippo. I found a phone book in a drawer and decided to call a limousine company.

Someone answered on the first ring. "This is Guido."

"Yeah, I need to hire a car for the evening. How fast can you get here?"

"Now, hold on." It sounded like Guido was sucking his teeth and settling in for a protracted negotiation.

"What?"

"Just how much are you thinking of paying?"

"Whatever you need. Get over here, pronto. The address—"

"Whoa, tiger, where's the fire? This your prom night?"

"Listen, Vinnie—"

"Guido."

"Who cares? I'm a homicide detective with a totaled car and I need to get to a murder scene fast. So whatever you need, combat pay, hazard pay, you got it. And you better start driving before I arrest you for being an asshole."

"Did they finally make that illegal?"

"Great, a driver and a comedian." I gave him the address and hung up. I returned to the living room, smiling smugly. "Okay, Marn, we're all set. A car will be here in about thirty minutes. Marny?" She was fast asleep on the couch, a few grains of rice stuck in her hair.

"Let her sleep, mate. She's had a hard day; she told us about her car," Alistair said.

"Everybody's days are hard right now," I said. "Look at us, cooped up here on top of each other, in sleeping bags, candles, and takeout."

"You don't like it, you can go home," Sophie said.

I thought of my dark, cold house with its electric stove, electric heat, electric hot water heater, no candles, no woman, and silence so thick it was cotton in my ears. I laughed crossly. "No, thanks."

I sat in an overstuffed wingback and stared at the fire until I heard a horn honk outside. "Don't wait up," I said as I gathered my wallet, keys, badge, gun, cigarettes, Zippo, flashlight, phone, and coat.

"Don't bring back any strange!" Sophie called.

I eased carefully down the sidewalk to the waiting bubblegum pink Hummer limo. Ice pellets pelted my scalp like a rain of needles. I sat in the front of the limo with the driver.

"Guido." He held out his hand.

"Jill," I said. "Don't you have anything less conspicuous?"

"Jill?" His eyes traveled from my flattop haircut to my masculine jaw to my flat chest to my slim hips to my Timberland boots. "Jill?" He repeated, ignoring my question about the vehicle's Pepto-Bismol color.

"Detective." I pressed. "Drive, moron."

"Lemme see your badge."

"Fuck off. Go!"

Guido put the car in park. "Now what about a little respect?"

"In a teenybopper car?" I removed my .40 caliber Glock from its shoulder holster and pointed it at Guido's head. "How's that?"

Guido started driving. "Good enough."

I reholstered my gun. "You didn't have any other vehicles?"

"Are you fucking kidding me? Forget about it. None of those fancy sedans could make the streets in this weather. This baby is the only one who eats ice and snow for breakfast." Guido patted the dash.

I grunted. We rode in silence.

"Some weather, huh?" Guido asked. "You got power yet?"

"No. Does anybody?"

"Not that I've heard. You know if those cocksuckers at the power company would bury the cables, this shit would never happen."

I grunted again. In an unpreventable natural disaster, everyone knew exactly what was wrong and how to fix it.

Finally, we arrived. There were six squad cars with their lights going and crime scene tape stretched around the yard's perimeter.

"Pull over here," I said. We were still half a block away. I didn't want everybody seeing this Hummer.

"Whaddya talk? Front door delivery! You don't want to walk a lot in this shit." Guido slid the car right up to the curb in front of the crime scene. "Fuck, you wasn't kiddin'." Guido seemed subdued and spooked. The fire trucks were leaving the scene.

"Civilians are not supposed to be here so pull on up the block and play with yourself until I get back. I don't know how long I'll be." I removed a roll of bills from my pocket. I peeled off two hundreds. "There's a down payment, okay?"

A gumshoe pulled open the door, anger contorting his face. "Move along, shitbag. Oh, Detective Rogers! I'm sorry. I thought it was…never mind. Need a hand?"

"No, I'm fine. Get out of my way." I slammed the door and Guido drove a short distance and parked.

"I always thought you were a gangsta pimp, and look! I won that office pool."

I ignored him and pulled my parka hood over my head and ran awkwardly for the house. "Smith, what do we have?" In the entryway, I stomped the ice off my boots and shook my coat.

"A pair of double taps. Attempted arson, but the fire put itself out."

"Nice when it does that for us. Execution?"

"For him maybe, but not her. The lady's in the bedroom and he's out here."

"Sexual assault on her?"

"Looks like."

"Witnesses?"

Smith laughed. "In this shit? No one is out. No one sees anything!" He looked out the living room window. "Is that your hot pink Hummer, Detective?"

"I rented it."

"Stick?"

"I don't know. Any other evidence around here? Shell casings, prints, what have you?"

"You don't know if it's a stick? You're not driving?"

"A driver came with. Who called in this crime?"

"Phew! I guess you hadn't heard that the city has a wage freeze, huh? I haven't gotten a raise in three years. And we haven't had a full police force since the hiring freeze in W's admin."

"Smith, go stand outside."

"What for, Detective?"

"Because I said so. Now."

"Fuckin' brassholes," Smith muttered as he slammed the door. I greeted Magnuson who had everything under control and was supervising the collection of fibers and prints.

I cautiously walked the scene, noting the man had been killed first, just as he entered the house from the garage. One shot, right in the brain. He never saw it coming. No sign of struggle. A single bullet and then the Dead Man's Fall. Whenever someone dies while standing, his feet cross and then he falls. People are all the same. I didn't know if it was a high or low caliber weapon or if the bullet was still in his brain, but I estimated an approximate trajectory and walked to the kitchen sink which was directly opposite the entry hall where the man was killed. There, in a cereal bowl lay the slug with bullet wipe on it, which is human blood seared to the bullet's surface. "Campbell," I called. "Tell Magnuson to make sure this is collected," I told him when he arrived.

He nodded. "Yes, sir." I patted Campbell's shoulder. I had long ago surrendered to being either a "sir" or a "ma'am" interchangeably.

I walked to the bedroom to view the woman. She was definitely the target. The scene was a real mess. "She fought," I said. She was naked, and there was a bloody claw hammer next to the bed. In the corner was a pile of crumpled, sodden newspapers the firemen had ensured was no longer flammable.

"Hey, Campbell?"

"Detective, sir?"

"I remember all my old cases and you know what this looks like to me?"

"No, sir."

"Bunny Jones," I said.

"That right, sir?"

"No forced entry. No burglary. Execution-style hit on the husband and sexual assault."

"Is he out of DOC already?" Campbell said.

"Uh, I don't know. Find out for me."

"Yes, sir."

I crept carefully around the scene, noting the wife's broken nails, the hair she had entwined in her lifeless fingers, the bruising on her thighs. I saw blood smear all over the lower half of her face, as if she had drunk from a bucket of blood. Her mouth was locked in a grimace, so I stepped close and pried open her mouth with my gloved fingers to see if I should be looking around the scene for missing teeth. I stared into the darkness of her mouth and I was startled back on my haunches. I couldn't believe what I saw. I shone my flashlight down her throat once more and confirmed. "Campbell?"

"Yes, sir?" He came running.

"Is that, in fact, a testicle?"

Campbell blanched and stared at the ceiling. "I don't know, sir."

"Okay, Marcie," I said, making a Peanuts reference I was sure he wouldn't understand, "*look* at it."

"I was just here to secure the perimeter. I'm sure the forensic people can—"

"See, Campbell, I'm a woman so I don't have any balls in spite of all my trying, so look at it!"

Campbell's eyes widened as he looked me over. "But Smith told me you were a man." He blushed. "I'm sorry, sir, I mean ma'am."

"Save it. It's a hazing all newbies get." I probed the vic's mouth with my gloved fingers and lifted the object slightly. Rigor mortis had set in and not yet released, so her jaw was locked in position.

"Don't! Don't take it out!" Campbell said. "I'm on the burg squad. I don't know about homicide evidence. I'll call someone."

"Campbell?" I shone my flashlight in his eyes. "You *do* have a pair, right? Then please verify."

Campbell moved extremely slowly toward the woman. He shone his flashlight for a millisecond into the woman's mouth. He nodded, turned green, cupped his crotch, and ran outside.

"Good for you," I told the woman. This will make finding the suspect really easy.

Campbell approached me, wiping his mouth. "I found out about Bunny."

"Yes?"

"Yeah, he got out six months ago."

"Still living at the same dump?"

"I was lucky to reach anyone at all and he didn't say. You got a hunch?"

"Could be. I'm headed over there anyway. Magnuson's got this." I returned to Guido and gave him another hundred and a new address.

"Are you serious?" Guido said, setting his jaw. "There's nothing but killers and dealers over there."

"Drive it like you stole it, man."

Guido carefully eased the Hummer limo into the well-worn ice ruts and cautiously crawled down the street.

"Fuck, your wipers are going faster than you are!" I lit a cigarette and inhaled to the center of my brain.

"No smok—nevermind," Guido said when I handed him another hundred. "This speed is just right for the conditions."

I glanced out the window. "I can walk faster than this."

"That's the first good idea you've had."

"Drive, pinhead."

"Guido."

"*Oh. My. God.* Step on it!"

"No one is going anywhere in this shit, Detective Jill. Whoever you're looking for will wait."

"Whomever." I corrected him absently and laughed. "You're right. I got a turd on the hook for suspicion of murder. He's heating up cocoa and salting the walk right now."

"You know that's not what I meant."

"Listen, if you're trying to flirt with me, no dice."

"Flirt! You're unbelievable. I wouldn't do you if you were the last pig on earth."

"Sure, I know, honey," I said in my finest patronizing tone. I saw Guido flush and he stomped on the accelerator. I braced myself against the jolting and grinned. We finally arrived at the mobile home park that was Bunny Jones's last known address.

I called dispatch for backup. Tammy, the night dispatcher, balked, but once I said Bunny Jones, she said she would send out everyone she could find, fast. I also instructed her to send a few recruits to canvas hospitals for this specific injury. No way would

Bunny try to self-doctor that in his mobile home latrine. Hydrogen and a Band-Aid wouldn't fix that.

Here's how I knew Bunny: he had a childhood so hard, it made kidnapping look good. After her husband took off, Bunny's mother stabbed his sister, drowned his brother, and poisoned Bunny with antifreeze. Bunny was already big and strong for his age of ten and survived the poisoning. He was taken into foster care, but returned to his home long enough to beat his mother to death with a claw hammer and set the house on fire. After that, he drowned his sorrows in every chemical concoction he could obtain and spent eight long years in and out of juvenile court.

Since then, I suppose Freud would say every woman wears his mother's face and he wants their love, hates them for it, and punishes all of them he can catch. I met him after Kendall and I investigated his first three murders.

"He does 'em all the same," Kendall said, "hammer and fire."

"I hope he gets death," I said.

"Best we can hope for is LWOP."

"Why?"

"Competency."

Kendall was right. Bunny was found incompetent, and instead of the needle, he got meds and time in an asylum and was recently released, but was on parole for the rest of his natural life. Bunny definitely was not smart, but he was cunning.

"You going in or what?" Guido asked.

I sucked my teeth. "You got somewhere to be?"

"No, I just wondered if...well, aren't you gonna...I mean, we're here. Why are you just sitting on your duff?"

"Didn't you just hear me call for backup?"

"Sure, but you was in such a hurry to get here, I thought you'd stomp in there, guns blazing."

"You watch *Law and Order*, don't you?"

"Doesn't everyone?"

"Stay low," I said as I opened the door and crept toward Bunny's dilapidated trailer, "and wait here." I stomped through the ice, wishing I had worn my hat to keep the ice off my head. The parka hood wasn't good enough. A few of the trailers had lights, and I heard the jet engine noise that indicated generators. Bunny's was one with power. I rapped on the door with my flashlight. A curtain parted. I rapped again. A distorted voice. I rapped once more.

"Who is it?" A man bellowed from behind the door.

"Your old friend, meth," I said.

"We ain't friends no more," came the answer.

"Crack?"

"Nope."

"Heroin? Coke?"

"Go away."

"Bunny, open the door."

"You got a warrant?" Was the muffled reply.

"Not yet, but I do have frozen assets. I just want to talk."

"My shit-eatin' lawyer ain't here with me."

"Good to know. Can I just come in to get warm?"

"Go back where you came from to warm up."

"Goddammit, Bunny! I will get a warrant if I have to, but Judge Kleinfelter is on duty and he will be so pissed to see me, he will make sure you burn for *something.*"

"Kleinfelter?" Bunny said. He opened the door. I rushed past him, rocking the trailer in my eagerness to be out of the ice.

"Thanks, Bunny." I shivered.

"You gotta go now," Bunny said. He had been nicknamed Bunny because he was so mean, even among the prison population. Apparently, convicts understood irony. He was my same height plus one hundred pounds. He only had one eye, and he hated wearing an eye patch because of the pirate jokes, so instead, I had to gaze at a little flesh fist where his eye should've been. His face was lined with ropy scars from multiple razor fights. He had a Celtic cross tattooed across his nose in the T-zone. Maybe to go with his Irish coloring, I thought wryly. And the word "DIE" tattooed below his lower lip.

"Already? I haven't had any coffee."

"You ain't gettin' none neither." Bunny hung his head and wouldn't look at me, but he moved to shove me out the door. He got too close, so on a wild impulse, I embraced him. Bunny gasped and flung me into the wall. "Don't do that." He still stared at his feet. "Go now."

"I'm sorry, Bunny. Come on. Let me stay. Of all the convicted murderers I know, you're my favorite."

Bunny's gaze flickered to mine for a flash. I saw a smile pull the edge of his lips.

"You've always been a big help to me. I could count on you no matter what. Please let me stay."

Bunny nodded then turned his back, walked to a battered recliner, and dropped into it like a load of stones. The trailer shuddered. I followed and perched on a coffee table. "So I just came from a homicide scene. Looked like your work. Did you do it?"

"Are you arresting me?" Bunny glared at me, his eye glittering. The dumb lug act was over. I wish the backup were here. They may never arrive. Sanding and salting the streets in this part of town was not even on the city's to do list in a disaster. Time for bravado.

"Maybe." I unsnapped my Glock holster. "Do I have reason to?"

Bunny laughed. "I just got out. I'm not goin' back." His gold tooth sparkled.

"Then help me, Bun. Do you know anything about this?"

"Don't forget to read me my rights."

"Goddammit, I'm not arresting you! This is just a chat."

"Okay, Detective…what are your hobbies?"

I sighed. This was going perfectly. What a brilliant cop I was. The lights went out. The sudden darkness was almost palpable. I stood up fast.

Bunny said in a slow drawl, "Relax, Jill. The generator just ran out of gas. Spooked you plenty, huh?" He laughed, his voice swirling in the black as the most menacing sound I'd ever heard. I tried to calm down. It's not an ambush. "I thought we was gonna talk."

"You want to play this game? I always win this game," I said as coolly as I could.

"Huh? What game?"

"Bunny, my man, if I pop you for this, you'll be buried so far under prison, you'll have to look up to see hell."

"Don't stress me, Jill. I go kinda cuckoo when I'm stressed. Let's just talk." I heard the click of some sort of gun in Bunny's hands.

"Well, Bunny, you don't seem to want to, so I'll just follow my other leads." I made my voice loud and bright. "Thanks a lot. You're a prince. See you around. Stay out of trouble." *Stop babbling!* I said to myself.

"Why did you think it was me, Jill?" Bunny's voice was sad but so dangerous.

"Lucky guess, Bun. If you're going to confess to something, I need to tell you that you have the right to remain silent—"

"It was a money gig." His voice was so low and menacing, like a shark's fin just visible above the water's surface and the real threat was right below.

"Anything you say or do can and will be used against you in a court of law."

"She wanted him gone. And I can't get a regular job, you know that!"

"You have the right to speak to an attorney," I continued doggedly.

"She hated her husband and wanted the insurance money." Voice like deadly gravel.

"If you cannot afford an attorney," I took a whopping breath to keep the words from rushing up my throat in a rapid panic.

"Met her through my ex, that lousy whore."

"One will be appointed to you."

"So I figure, now this gal is single. I helped her out; she should help me out."

"Do you understand these rights…"

"She didn't want to. Don't you hate when you're goin' along swell, something goes wrong, and you have to kill her?"

"As they have been read to you?" I was feeling for my cuffs and my cell. "Bunny?"

"Huh?"

"Yes or no?"

"Yes, I've got you here, and no, you're goin' nowhere." His laugh rang out like shotgun blasts. My scalp jumped and my skin crawled. Maintain, I told myself. "Bunny, don't make it hard on yourself. You're in police custody now."

"Nope." I heard the recliner squeal as he stood. I heard ice beads tapping the windows. "You're in Bunny custody now."

"Bunny, don't make it worse."

"It wasn't me. I swear I'm bein' framed."

In the darkness, my cynicism overtook my nerves and I rolled my eyes. "That right, Bun? Who did it, then?"

"You crazy? I can't tell a pig."

"No, I understand. You can't tell a pig. But you can tell me. I won't tell anyone. I promise."

Everything went silent and still. I heard ice pellets hitting the trailer like buckshot.

"Really?" Bunny's sudden gullibility made me feel briefly guilty. "You won't tell?"

"Sure thing, Bunny. You know me. I ain't one of them. I'm just curious. The chief can go fuck himself. I'm no rat."

"You wear a goddamn badge! You arrested me. You testified against me and sent me to the looney bin."

"Yeah, but…"

"But what?" Bunny waited. I could feel his expectation. The promise of an opening if I said the right thing.

"Listen, Bun," I said, my voice warm and sweet like cocoa. "Jesus is my Lord and Savior and everything I do every day is for His Glory." The false words slid out easily from extensive practice. "As a child of the Lord, I am always seeking to do what is right."

Bunny snorted.

Undaunted, I continued. "I see you, Bunny. Underneath all that," I felt around for a chair and located a rickety wooden stool and sat, "you're sweet and tender with a golden heart."

Bunny laughed, but I could tell this was the right way to go. This strategy never worked on smart suspects, but it worked like magic on the dummies and those riddled with superstition and faith. My fellow detectives called this interrogation routine my "old reliable."

"You've been hurt," I said. "No one was there to give you the care," I punched my fist into my palm, "and hell, the *justice* you deserved."

Bunny sighed, his breath ragged.

"And I know you're a righteous man and you want to see justice done when you can help. You can rely on God's Love, Bunny. Jesus loves you. Yes, he does. No matter what," I paused for the big finish, making my voice low and kind, "and *I love you.*"

"The hell you say," Bunny whispered.

"Of course I do. You're a beloved child of the Lord and you are hungry for salvation. And you love Jesus. I know that. How could I not love a fellow sinner, searching for righteous truth, just like me?"

Bunny laughed. "Swear. Swear on…" Bunny fumbled in the dark. "My hammer."

"Your…?" My voice dropped off the edge of the earth.

"Swear, Jill." I felt Bunny come close. When he found me, he pushed a cold claw hammer into my gut. I tried to take it, but Bunny held it fast. "Swear," he repeated.

"I swear, Bunny."

He moved away and I heard him sit in his recliner again. "It was Dwayne and Wayne. They tried to get me to do the job, but I didn't want to. I just got home. So they did it and made it look like me."

"Dwayne and Wayne, huh? Think they might still be in town?"

"Why, Jill?" Bunny heaved himself up again and lumbered toward me.

I tripped and fell in a heap on the smelly shag carpeting. I was a goddamned arrogant son of a bitching fool. What was I thinking, coming here by myself like some rogue superhero? I had been disciplined for it in the past. "Bullet vests won't fix stupid," I had been told. "Bunny!" I commanded masterfully. "You are under arrest. I will repeat your rights to you."

"Jill, Jill, Jill..." Bunny whispered. "Didn't you hear? I'm not going back." Bunny's voice was like a spider's.

"Bun Bun, a gun is a permanent solution to a temporary problem."

"DOC ain't temporary."

"You have the right to remain silent." I crab walked around the floor, bumping into furniture and still seeking my cuffs and phone.

"Cut the shit," Bunny said. "You promised! So we can do this the easy way or the hard way."

"Aw, Bunny, don't be that guy." I boomed, faking jocularity and standing up.

"Easy or hard." I felt a crushing grip around my throat from behind.

"You know me," I wheezed. "I always go the hard way." I speared my elbow into his solar plexus and he let go with a gasp. I couldn't see where he or the door was, but in my stumbling, I kicked my cuffs out of my reach, and with a loud crunch, knew I had killed my phone. "That fucker always needed charging anyway," I said.

Bunny couldn't see in the dark any better than I, and I didn't want to turn on my flashlight and help him find me. I had no phone, no cuffs, and no backup yet. I could shoot him, but I only wanted to do that as a last resort. I felt Bun's hot, hard hand like an iron knock me in the face in his search. I fell against the door. I reached behind myself and unlatched the door, and just as Bunny lunged, opened the door and we both fell out of the trailer, down the steps, and onto the ice. Bunny was trying to get on top. I rolled and got him in a squirmy and barely contained half nelson. I saw Guido leaning against the limo, staring open-mouthed and frozen at this spectacle. A cigarette smoldered, forgotten, in his hand. I heard sirens approaching. I prayed they were close enough.

"Guido!" I shrieked. "Tell them officer down!" Bunny broke my grip and towered over me. "Officer down!" I screamed, reaching for my Glock. I pointed it at Bunny's head. "Don't move, shitbird."

After turning Bunny over for processing on A & B on a police officer, I returned to the crime scene. There was something missing. Headquarters called. Bunny had both his balls, so this really wasn't him. I missed something and I needed to get lucky and find whatever that was.

CHAPTER TWENTY

The scene was still lurid with generators and floodlights and police tape and cruisers parked so their headlights shone to light the scene.

They had secured the house and yard and the thousand square yards of field behind the house. I had spoken to the first responders, and they only guessed at taping off the field because there was no evidence to suggest how the killer left. The ice was so thick and hard that footprints and tire prints just didn't show up.

I left the team to wrap up and I just started walking. I removed my right leather glove so I could light my Zippo, which was key to my detective skills. I began by walking around the outside of the house. I know the team had already looked, but this was a hunch and part of my process, so I inspected windows and shrubbery and sidewalks and garage doors and rooflines. My flashlight was losing power, so I borrowed a fresh one from a rookie. Then I walked the perimeter of the yard, flicking my Zippo with my right hand and sweeping the light beam with my left. The ice underfoot was iron hard, but rough, so it wasn't slick. I found a pair of luxury dogs shivering in a pile of brush. They had been tied to the fence and their snouts were bound with duct tape.

I knelt, removed my Swiss army knife from my pocket, sliced off the tape, cut the leashes, and gathered the terrified dogs into my coat. They shivered and whined. I was surprised they just hadn't been shot outright, which is what usually happened to animals at a crime scene.

I carried the dogs to the house where the last officers were overseeing the coroner as he removed the bodies.

"Look what I found." I presented the dogs by unzipping my coat and their heads, matted with ice, poked out.

"Bichon and Llasa!" Officer Magnuson said, coming close to hold them.

"You know their names?" I asked.

"No, genius, they're purebred," Magnuson said as he picked ice balls out of the fur between their toes. "I have some just like this. I'll take them home."

"Good man." I clapped him on the shoulder. Thank goodness there were so many animal lovers because death by accident, homicide, suicide, or natural causes, resulted in a lot of suddenly homeless and frequently traumatized animals that had to be euthanized after spending a sad week at the shelter.

I returned to the spot where I had found the dogs and noticed some fibers on the privacy fence. I called for an investigator to collect that as evidence while I climbed over the fence and dropped to the other side. Even dropping six feet from the top of the fence didn't break the ice on impact.

I walked the perimeter of the field, not finding anything further. But my Zippo said to go for the woods. So I chose a likely trail and kept walking. About half a mile in, I saw blood. I radioed for backup and had to put my Zippo back in my pocket so I could approach with my Glock drawn.

It was completely silent. I checked behind trees, under piles of brush and in crevices. Finally, under a rotten log, I found the man.

"Hands where I can see them!" I said.

He was curled in a fetal position and didn't move. I crept closer until I could prod him with my boot. I reached for the radio on my collar again. "This is Rogers. Cancel the backup. Bring a body bag."

The man looked like a meth head, which is probably how he vaulted the fence without leaving more evidence. His pants seemed to be stuffed with every towel ever made.

He froze or died of blood loss or both. I waited until the team found me.

"You're one lucky sumbitch, Rogers. You did it again," Officer Smith said.

I shrugged and smiled. "I do what I do." I reholstered my Glock and lit a cigarette and walked back to Guido and the Hummer.

CHAPTER TWENTY-ONE

A m I gonna have to put you on desk duty, Detective?" Chief St. John said. We were sitting in his car outside Sophie's house. The ice had not let up. Every few seconds, the wipers cleared a thick slushy mass from the windshield. Chief was pissed. He called me "detective" when he thought I fucked up. Otherwise, it was Jilldo.

"Got my man, didn't I?"

"Detective Rogers! Would you like to return to the academy to relearn what never to do?"

"No, sir."

"Do you need to take remedial cop?"

"No, sir."

"Are you, in fact, a retard?"

"Maybe, sir."

"Do you find this funny, 'tard?"

"Little bit."

"Maybe you need to be suspended until you shake out your sillies."

"*Chief,* Bunny is as crazy as a clown's dick!"

"What the fuck does that have to do with anything?"

I held my head, exhausted, discouraged. "I got him," I said.

"Is this a game to you? Are you indulging the cowboy impulses?"

"No, sir, it just works out that way."

Chief St. John rubbed his eyes, also exhausted. "He's asking for you."

I chuckled. "That Bunny."

The chief nodded, his head back, his eyes closed.

"Well, let's go." I fastened my seat belt.

Chief laughed harshly. "Get in the house and don't come out until tomorrow."

"Can I have my gun and badge back?" I reached. "Sir?"

Chief St. John handed them to me as if they weighed fifty pounds. He shook his head. "How are things with Perryman?"

"We're working together on Goodson."

"Fine. Stay out of her pants, Jilldo. That's an official departmental order."

"You can't do that!"

"Is there any order at all that you'll follow?" Chief St. John looked so old.

"I'll throw you a bone on this. She's not my type."

Chief sighed. "Thanks. Now take a day off."

"Also an order?"

"Does it have to be?"

"Yes."

"Fuck you, Jilldo. If you weren't so good; I'd fry you."

"Love you too." I stepped out of the car and wobbled up to Sophie's front door. The ice pecked my eyes. I didn't have my key. I knocked. Marny, in a quilted robe, let me in.

"Any Chinese left?" I stomped into the living room, rubbing and blowing on my hands. "I'm famished."

Perryman sat next to the fire, holding a tissue to her nose. Marny shrugged. "It's fucking Grand Central," she said, her voice hoarse. "All we need is a judge and a PD and we can run court."

"Where's Sophie?" I asked.

"She and Alistair are in bed."

Asleep? I almost asked, still hoping he was her brother. I nodded and knelt in front of the sheriff. "Dana? What happened?"

"It's Wanda. She's dead." She wept softly.

Marny crunched an egg roll. "What's a Wanda, your dog?" She stirred a martini with her eggroll and ate it.

"My daughter-in-law!" Perryman said.

"How? When?" My spine was touched with an electric wire.

"Gunshot and mutilated. We found part of her tonight. Oh, God, why? Why?"

"Exactly how *old* is this daughter-in-law? I don't know anyone named Wanda under sixty," Marny said, finishing her drink and gathering food containers.

"Do you want me to go with you anywhere?" I asked.

Perryman shook her head. "We're having her cremated instead of buried because of the ice."

I nodded. "You want to bed down here?"

"No, I've got to be with my son. I just couldn't reach you by phone, and I thought since we're working together on Goodson, we can work together on this."

"Sure, baby, sure thing." I pulled her to standing and hugged her. "Are you okay to drive?"

"Yeah, takes my mind off of it. Call me tomorrow?"

"Can't. Phone is broken and I won't have a new one until the thaw."

"I have to be able to reach you!" Perryman said.

"I know, I know," I said. Perryman was becoming a sexless girlfriend. All demands and no fun.

"Get a pre-paid." Marny suggested from under the blankets on the couch.

"Yeah, listen, I'll do that. First thing."

"Buy a car," Marny said.

"Right. Fuck, I need a car. Well, don't worry. I'll fix it and we will talk tomorrow. Need a sleep aid?" I held up a bottle of scotch.

"Sure, I'll take anything." Perryman took a long swallow from the bottle without flinching and then put the cap back on and marched bravely outside, clutching the scotch like a baby.

I heard Marny's light snore, and I felt comforted to be in a house full of people. We were all together, seeing this through. I crept down the hall to Sophie's bedroom. I heard Alistair's breathing so I opened the door and stared longingly at the small berm in the bed.

I wanted to creep, ice-cold, to that king-sized paradise and ease myself in to be welcomed by a blood-warm coziness. To be embraced by mouth, arms, breasts, belly, hips, and legs. To feel Sophie's life-warmth join us and spread to me, saving me, healing me. To melt into her parted thighs and to dissolve into her sex. To feel her breath on my neck, reassuring me that everything was okay. To place my hand on her tummy and feel the calm, deep breathing that made me secure. To nest under the blankets in a sacred tangle of limbs. To be held fast—making me whole, grounding me to the beauty of this earth, to feel absolute love, as if we were twins in the womb, swimming in joy and pillows.

Alistair stirred and drew Sophie close to him, nuzzling her and nesting her back against him. She cooed in response. I could almost feel the carved muscle of her back, the heavy weight of breast, the rise of her hip, the plump curve of her buttocks, the relaxed beat of her heart. My eyes stung, and I closed the door quickly, returned to the fire in the living room, and sat up all night, nursing my allergies on bourbon.

CHAPTER TWENTY-TWO

The next day, I rode in Sophie's car as she took me to get a phone. I was glad it was a deeply gray day because the sun would've made my head explode.

I lit a Camel, and at Sophie's piercing glance, I lowered the window. She snapped the heat on high.

"Want one?" I held the box out to her. I could see my breath, but no matter how cold it was, I had to smoke. Zippo open, closed, open, closed.

"What do you think, genius?'

"What's stuck up your vag?" I said.

"Fuck you."

"What the hell is this chicksand?"

"You've driven Alistair away. He's leaving as soon as the airport reopens."

"What? Me? I like the guy. You did good." I slugged her on the shoulder.

"Alistair dumped me." Sophie swerved the bucking car over the deep ice grooves and slammed it into park. She turned the highest volume of fury on me—full face. "We'll always be *friends,* thank you."

"Well, at least you're a good loser," I said.

"Show me a good loser and I'll show you a loser," she said.

"When did this happen?"

"Last night."

I started to protest by saying "when I spied on you, you were happily spooning," but I stopped myself in time. "What brought this on? You two were fine!"

"Nothing worth noting." Sophie sniffed, turning to look forward again. "He said that I wasn't in love with him."

"Well, are you?"

"Of course!" Sophie said.

"I guess you're not that convincing." I shrugged and flicked my butt out the window where it sizzled briefly. "Can we go? I have calls to make."

"He says I'm in love with someone else."

My eyes dilated and my heart thumped. I felt the veins in my neck pulsing. I slowly unbuckled my seat belt and turned to Sophie, who clung to the steering wheel and stared miserably at the road. I embraced her, folding her body into mine as much as I could in the car. "Of course you're in love with someone else," I whispered huskily. She held on to me tightly. Finally. There was some great click in the universe and inside me. At last, the right, true, and proper thing was happening. "Oh, Sophie, Sophie," I sighed. "You're all I've ever wanted. You're the only one—"

"Shut up," she said.

I lowered my mouth onto hers and then jerked away. "Did you hear that?" I looked around.

"What?" Sophie seemed drugged and happy.

"Bells," I said. Sophie smiled so sweetly that I felt tears tickle the corners of my eyes, and I returned to her mouth for nourishment. "Who cares about a goddamn phone?" I murmured to her lips. In reply, Sophie wrenched herself from me and drove back to her house, her lustful speed making the ride feel like bumper cars.

We ran up the sidewalk together. Once, I slipped and fell and Sophie helped me up. Then she slipped and fell and as I tried to lift her, I fell again. We laughed; we struggled to rise; we kissed; we laughed and kissed more. Sophie's eyes were dark with longing.

She pushed my coat down around my waist. I watched as she began removing her clothes. Sophie was down to her bra and jeans before I snapped to.

"Goddamn it, woman! Don't do that here! Get in the house." I finally stood securely and lifted Sophie. I gathered her clothes into a bundle and clapped them to her chest. She didn't clasp them to her but let them fall. I stared in amazement at her red lace demi cup bra as if it were a cobra and I a mongoose.

"What now?" I managed to say.

"Jill." Sophie's voice was grave. Serious enough to make me look at her face. "This has to happen. I've waited too long. Do you understand?"

I shrugged dismissively. "The only thing between us now is that house key."

"I mean it." Sophie's face was mean and merciless. "I can't go through all that again." I moved to caress and reassure her, but Sophie flinched.

"Baby," I said, and at her murderous stare. I said, "Sophie, ain't no one between us. I'm all yours if you want me."

"I do," she said, her manner as grave as if she were identifying a corpse.

"Can we go in?" I tried to pull her arm.

"Finally, you and me. It's real?" Sophie seemed dazed.

"Will you at least put on your coat?" I tried to wrap her, but she swatted me.

"I'm going inside. Care to join me?" I walked to the stoop. Sophie picked up her clothes as if she were underwater and floated to stand next to me. She dropped her clothes again and crushed me to her. She caught my mouth in a deep, delicious kiss and caught me off balance and we fell again, but we didn't laugh.

The front door burst open, and Alistair stood there. "What the bloody hell is going on?" He took in the sight of us as we scrambled to stand. Sophie still didn't cover herself even though her skin was swollen with goose bumps. So I held her coat up like a curtain.

"The body is not even cold yet," Alistair said.

"Alistair—" Sophie started, "you were right—"

"Sod off!" Alistair slammed the door and the deadbolt.

"You know why this is funny?" Sophie turned to me, her face solemn but on the verge of laughter.

"For God's sake, put your fucking clothes on!" I shouted. The sound carried through the silent ice-encrusted neighborhood like a gunshot.

"Well, this isn't the proper direction of seduction," Sophie mused. "What's the big deal? This"—she gestured to her plump, taut breasts—"is like a bikini top. I didn't know you were so uptight." She slid into her coat. I zipped it up to her chin. "I don't have my key."

My eyebrows rose. "Say what now?"

"So we will have to beg or call a locksmith."

"You're right. That's hilarious," I said.

"Come on, you can't blame him," Sophie said.

"Like hell!" I banged on the door. "Come on, Al, don't be a dick!" My voice boomed through the soundless white landscape like a timpani. In response, ice slid off someone's roof and exploded in frigid shards and a tree limb finally gave out and crashed to the ground.

"Let me try." Sophie stroked the door as if it were silk. "Alistair, honey," she crooned. "Alistair, it's not you; it's me. Alistair, ducks… come on, please? I'm sorry…truly and really sorry. If I had my way, I wouldn't give a shit about this tool; it would be you forever. But I can't explain my heart and I can't help it."

"Hey, wait a minute," I said.

"Sh!" Sophie hissed. "Alistair, dear, please let us in. It's cold and I have to use the bathroom. Come on, nutmeg."

"Nutmeg?" I echoed sourly.

"Shut up," she snapped. Then sweetly, "Alistair, don't do this. Remember Rio? Remember Amsterdam? Come on, please?"

"You went to Rio and Amsterdam?" I asked. Sophie ignored me. I brushed her aside and hit the door so hard my hand stung.

"Don't be this guy!" I yelled. Then to Sophie, "I don't have a phone to call a locksmith. I will shoot the door open." I unsnapped my holster.

"You will not!" Sophie shouted. "Alistair, Jill's going to shoot the door open. Please open it or step aside."

"How do I always end up in these embarrassing dramas?" I said, flicking off the safety and taking aim. The door jerked open and Alistair grabbed Sophie, yelled, "bugger off!" into my face, and pulled Sophie with him back into the darkness and slammed and locked the door again.

I reholstered my Glock. I would sleep out here before I would shoot now. I kicked the door. "We're not going to have a *situation*, are we, buddy?"

"Jill! I'm all right!" came Sophie's muzzy voice. "Just give us some time."

I walked to the sidewalk steps and sat, marveling at how different the circumstances were between this episode of being locked out of Sophie's and just a few days ago, in this same ice storm when I had been a pathetic loser, rabid with longing, sitting here with my bumped head and broken heart, trying to accept the loss. Now I was supposed to be with Sophie, yet I was still locked out. Yep, I laughed to myself, I've come full circle and haven't moved an inch.

They could be reconciling in there! I panicked and ran to the door. "Stand back!" I yelled. "I'm going to kick in the door!" A couple walking home, their arms laden with grocery sacks, stared curiously.

"Not bloody likely," Sophie said from the other side of the door, doing a damn good impression of Alistair. "It's a steel door in a steel frame. Just calm your randy ass down and give us a motherfucking minute!"

"Why? Are you making a soufflé?" I said and then grinned and waved at the couple, who walked on.

The door opened an inch. "He's crying!" Sophie said.

I rolled my eyes. "That's the oldest trick in the book!"

"Go smoke. Or better yet, take a drive." Sophie pushed the keys through the crack.

"Go for a drive? Are you kidding me?"

"Do what you want; I don't care. I have my hands full with this mess." She started to close the door, but I stopped it with my palm.

"Sophie," I said as solemnly as she had earlier, "this has to happen."

"Yeah, sure, whatever." Sophie locked the door.

CHAPTER TWENTY-THREE

I got in the Volvo and backed into the street. Sophie's cell was on the passenger seat. I called the chief at home. "It's Rogers. Do you know where Sheriff Perryman lives? I heard about her daughter-in-law and I'm on my way over there."

"Don't try to comfort her with sex."

"Well, I'm all out of casseroles."

"Then get her flowers."

"From outta my bum? Pull a bouquet out of my arse?" I could imitate Alistair too.

"Send her a card."

"Come on, Chief," I said, caressing my Zippo like the talisman it was. He relented, as usual, and looked up the address and read it to me. West side. I turned the car around and drove west. The clouds were breaking up. They thinned and scattered, with hints of forgotten porcelain blue sky. The sun was weak, the temperature remained below freezing, and none of the ice was melting, but the light was penetrating and over bright as if the entire town had been hiding in a movie theater and had been pushed onto the brilliant sidewalk mirrored with ice. As I got on the highway, I saw a convoy of power trucks trundling by. I was tempted to follow them and buy a house wherever they fixed the electricity. But a grieving Perryman expecting my call kept me on course.

The highway had only one lane open—two treacherous tracks right in the middle. On either side, the road was clogged with untouched ice like a turbulent ocean of white topped with a thin, craggy, glacier crust.

Since Perryman's number wasn't in Sophie's phone, I couldn't call ahead. Oh, well. I finally arrived at a long, Ranch-style brick home with white columns and shutters. There was a thick forest looming behind the house, and it appeared to be shoving the home forward. The front porch light was on. The driveway seemed to be groaning under its load of SUVs.

I knew this was the sort of house that one only used the back door to enter. And I wouldn't knock, either. It would vex them and set me apart if I did.

So I slid the glass door and walked into the heat and noise. The TV was on and there were half a dozen deputies sat in recliners and a pit group watching a game. There were bowls of nuts and chips within arm's reach of anyone. On the glass coffee table was an impressive pyramid of beer cans, and the big screen was wall mounted so the can construction didn't interfere with their viewing.

Four children chased each other over my feet—one on a Big Wheel, one on a tricycle, one on a hoppity horse, and one carrying a pogo stick.

All the lights, the noise, the warmth…I didn't hear a generator. Where was Perryman? No one noticed me. I took off my coat and got a beer. As I was savoring the last ice-cold swallow, Perryman came in, wiping her hands.

"Detective!" She exclaimed. All heads swiveled to me. "What are you doing here?" She threw down the towel, fumbling for her phone. "Did I miss a message? Do we have a meeting?"

"Nope, just wanted to drop in."

Everybody relaxed and forgot me again. It's funny how I can so easily read the level of prickly tension in a room caused by my presence and at what exact moment that melted. When it doesn't, I have a problem.

"Well, that's very thoughtful…I guess…want a beer?"

I crumpled my can and resisted the overpowering impulse to lob it into the pyramid and see it topple. "Had one." I belched.

"Another then?"

"Sure."

"How long have you been here?"

"Hours and hours." I replied as I snapped open my beer.

"Well?" Perryman seemed nervous that I was on her home turf.

"Football?" I asked, already hypnotized.

"Yeah, we got power yesterday. Nothing has been off for one second since. All the deputies have gone without TV and football for so long, and I'm the first with power restored. I think they used the excuse of Wanda's murder to come over here to watch the game and pretend to support me. I'm just in shock, so I really don't care." Perryman rubbed her face. The kids made another circuit of the kitchen.

"Yours?" I said.

"No, some of the various deputies' kids. They're too young to know what's going on."

"Well, do you have any leads?"

"It's such a relief having power," Perryman said as if I hadn't asked. She seemed stiff and awkward.

I stared at her in puzzled disbelief. Then, "well…" I belched again into my fist. "Wanna tell me about Wanda?"

Perryman wiped the nose of the boy with the pogo stick. She hugged her elbows. "No, not really. I'll look into the leads I've got and I'll be in touch."

I finished the beer and stomped the can flat. I shrugged. "Well, that's why I'm here."

Perryman's eyes narrowed and her neck reddened. "You mean *officially?*"

I snorted. "No. Why would I need to be here officially?" My radar was up. Something here was off. Perryman was such a dynamo, her reluctance with her own daughter-in-law's murder was a red flag. If I stuck around, maybe something would shake loose. I might overhear something.

"It's a homicide. You're a homicide detective aren't you?"

Zippo out. Click. Click. Tread lightly. "Not until the thaw. Got any Cheetos?"

Perryman absently handed me a bowl piled with a lovely dome of space age orange curls. She chewed her thumbnail.

"Got any theories?" I asked extremely casually.

Perryman seemed absent and preoccupied. "Oh, you know. Harris and Gerritts and I all agree. It's her drug connections."

"Drug connections?" I crunched on a handful of Cheetos. I needed to seem as if I believed every word and agreed with her. "I'm sure you're right on that. Dealers aren't anyone you ever want to mess with."

"Yeah, so we will probably never solve it," Perryman said and sniffled.

My eyebrows went up and I dropped my gaze to the Cheeto bowl, sorting through the curls, looking for the cheesiest ones. "Odds are against us, that's for sure."

"Poor Dewey." Perryman began crying silently. She turned away.

"Mind if I watch the game?" I asked.

"No, go ahead." Perryman disappeared before she finished answering.

I approached the men. "What's the score?" The standard male opener.

"Twenty-seven, twenty-one."

"Hey, scooch over, will ya?" I sat on the chaise section of the pit group. Next thing I knew, I was being shaken awake by Perryman. My hand was down the front of my trousers, and I had a taffy string of drool oozing from my mouth to my shoulder. Jonathan was licking Cheeto crumbs off my fingers. The TV was blaring another game, but it was dark outside. All the deputies around me were draped like snoring apes over the furniture.

"Whazzup, baby?" I rubbed my eyes and sat upright.

"Go on home now. You don't live here. This is family time."

"What about these guys?" I gestured to the snoring deputies.

"They'll be leaving too. It's just my son and me and we need private time."

"Sure." I stood and stretched, still groggy. "I don't have a phone yet."

"So I won't expect your call," Perryman said. "Let me walk you out."

"All right, all right." My fingers on my other hand were still Day-Glo orange. "Can I wash my hands?"

Perryman's jaw tightened; her lips pressed into a white line. She fished a tissue square out of her bra, spat on it, grabbed my stained paw, and scrubbed it. I was too dozy to protest. A young man of about twenty-three appeared in the door. His hair was a wild mess and his eyes were red. He picked Jonathan up and nuzzled him. "Mommy?" The young man asked so mournfully that my heart cracked a little and I almost embraced him. Perryman dropped my hand and turned me brusquely toward the door.

"That's it," she ordered, "good-bye."

"Is that your son?" I asked to the locked door. Jonathan ran out the cat door after me, sure-footed and frisky on the ice.

CHAPTER TWENTY-FOUR

On the slick, treacherous drive back to Sophie's, I heard that telltale sound of sand sifting onto the car.

"No! No! No!" I screamed, turning the wipers on frenzy speed as if they could reverse the weather. I screamed "no" for the entire trip.

I knocked on Sophie's door, wondering if I would have to sleep in the car. I don't need this hassle, I thought. Maybe it was time to go home.

Past time to go, I amended as Sophie opened the door wearing only a red lace bra, red panties, and après ski boots.

"Where the fuck have you been?" Sophie snapped, jerking me inside and brushing ice chips off my flattop.

"What the fuck are you wearing?" I said, my voice cracked and hoarse from shouting at the ice.

"Sh! We talked, he drank a couple of Guinesses, and now he's sleeping."

"That's a long explanation, but it doesn't answer why you're dressed like an alpine whore."

"And you are just using evasion to avoid telling me where you've been. Let me smell your hands." She moved toward me and I automatically pocketed.

"Let me smell yours," I countered.

Her mouth tightened like a knot in a balloon and her eyes glittered with fury. "Well, Jill, that's just fine. I told you, I can't go through your psychotic hot and cold attitudes and I won't. You need to pack your shit and go."

"I'll explain if you'll explain. You'll laugh when you hear it."

"I did explain!" Sophie said.

"Sh! Sophie's precious boyfriend is having a nippy nap."

"Fuck you. At least I clean up my messes."

"What the hell do you mean by that?"

Sophie stood up tall, her breasts righteous. "You want me to get specific?"

I rolled my eyes. "No. I've had enough of your specifics. Keep 'em. I've got a gut full. I give. Now will you take me home?"

Sophie looked crestfallen. "What about us?"

I shrugged. "I don't think it's a good idea until Rumpole of the Bailey leaves. It's in poor taste."

"You douchebag!" Sophie screamed, launching herself at me. "How dare you? I was going to be the one to say no, let's wait! How do you always do that?" She pummeled me with her fists, and I grabbed around the waist, hoisted her onto my shoulder, and carried her to the living room. I dumped her on the couch.

"Fine." I snapped, throwing my coat in a corner and whipping off my holster and belt. I stripped off my shirt and began unzipping my trousers. "Let's do it right here, right now. Gimme all ya got. Make me cry." Sophie placed a well-aimed kick at my crotch. "Damn, girl, you want it rough?" I grabbed her wrists and was about to cuff her like a suspect when I saw the tears dropping down her face.

"I'm going to bed," Sophie said, brushing past me; contempt shrouded her like perfume. I almost choked on the smell. I dropped wearily onto the couch, willing my mind blank. As smooth and untroubled as a virgin sheet of ice. I stared into the fire so long, my eyes watered. To rein that in, I clicked and caressed the Zippo one million times. I heard footsteps approaching.

"Hello, mate," Alistair said, sitting next to me.

"So we're cool?" I asked.

"Damn sorry about that." Alistair chortled and ran his hands through his hair. "Quite mortified about it. Can we just pretend it never happened?"

"Pretend what never happened?"

"Splendid."

"So, airline food, what's up with that, huh? And what about the drivers in this town? Are they nutty or what?"

Alistair laughed sadly. "I see why she loves you."

"Hey, man, one at a time, all right?'

"She called your name."

The hairs on the back of my neck prickled. "Alistair, listen…"

"There's no way to pass off Jill as any sort of Alistair derivative."

"I'm sorry."

"She's way too good for you, isn't she?" Alistair squinted at me. "So I ran amok for a bit and now I got myself in hand again. The stiff upper lip and all that."

I didn't know what to say so I said, "I don't know what to say."

"Quite."

"Offering tea seems to be the English way. Would it help?"

"It might do."

"Care for a cup? I could put in a rain barrel of liquor."

Alistair laughed again. "Rather. But not at the moment."

CHAPTER TWENTY-FIVE

I sensed Alistair wanted me to sit with him and help draw out the poison of the pain, so I leaned down and scavenged through several empty pizza boxes until I found one with leftovers. I picked up a slice that was as cold and stiff as frozen leather and began eating.

"I miss England," Alistair said wistfully, staring hard at the flames. "I hate Oklahoma."

I laughed. "That's easy to do."

"Too right."

"So really, you're not losing anything to go home," I said. "You're doing yourself a favor. Oklahoma isn't worth it."

Alistair grinned and nodded. "You do have a bloody good point."

"Hell, yeah." We bumped fists.

"You know what I'll miss though?" He asked softly. I tightened my muscles, preparing for the soliloquy about Sophie. Her curly hair, glossy and shimmering like waving sun-warmed wheat. Her smile, like hope in spring, her arms that fit around you and snapped in place as precisely as Legos, both your parts inserting and receiving like Tinker Toys, your legs locking in harmony like Lincoln Logs, building something sturdy and real. I wondered, feeling swords in my stomach, if Alistair would regale me with Sophie's lovemaking. Were there sighs or did she pant and moan? Did she close her eyes or stay open for everything? Surely she preferred complete and utter nudity because lingerie would be absurd. Like putting a tacky muumuu on Venus.

"The humor," Alistair said.

I had to shake my head to clear from it cherubic visions of glorious pure nudity and pulchritudinous thighs and pendulous breasts and ample bellies and chewy fat bottoms, all embracing and yielding to me. I cleared my throat. "The humor?"

"Take your Judge Gilbert. I observed a burglary trial where he gave the defendant five thousand years."

"I heard about that. Funny as hell. Didn't the guy have an extensive second page?"

"He had fifteen previous burglary convictions; he had been released from prison the week before, and when he was arrested, he was drunk and holding an axe. The victim came home and found him."

"Yep, that is rich!" I agreed. "But still, Brittania…"

"And there was another district court case during sentencing in which the judge instructed the jury to write a 'one' on a piece of paper and to then write zeroes and keep writing until their hands got tired."

"I remember that! Afterward, the defense attorney told me that it was an incredible victory just to get 567 years."

Alistair snorted. "See? You don't have mavericks like that in England."

"Did you ever see that ADA Fred Winston?" I asked.

"The one with the eyeball? No, I have heard of his antics."

"That's right. He would've been before your time; he retired right before you arrived. Well, he was a really passionate guy. Superhero complex. You know, a fire and spit kinda guy. Well, he also had a glass eye, and I don't know anything about them, but I guess they come in sizes? Anyway, old Fred would really get a righteous sermon going, and that glass eye would fly out of his skull like a boiled egg shot from a stunt cooch. Well, that old boy Fred wouldn't miss a beat, and he would just pick up that eyeball and put it right back in and keep going."

"That's nonsense!" Alistair laughed, looking happy.

"Nope. Saw it happen many times. He always won his cases. Really impressed juries. Finally, Judge James ordered him to see a doctor about it. Forced him to have it fixed. Thought it was prejudicial."

Alistair leaned back, giggling and glowing in the firelight. "Yes, I will miss this."

"But just think…now you can tell these stories yourself."

"To the wonder and delight of all England, eh?"

"Well…"

"As you say, you're quite right, you know."

We sat in silence and finally drifted off to sleep. My insomnia wasn't so bad in Sophie's house. I was sleeping better during this ice storm visit than I had in my whole career.

CHAPTER TWENTY-SIX

When I woke up, I was stiff and alone. My mouth was filled with morning slime. How long had it been since I brushed my teeth? I smelled breakfast and wandered into the kitchen. Alistair was there wearing a frilly apron over his parka and scrambling eggs in one skillet and home fries in another.

"Morning," I mumbled.

"Good morning. Care for some tea?"

"No. Want a smoke?" I held out an American Spirit.

"What the hell." I perched the extra cigarette on Alistair's lip and Zippoed it as he kept jiggling the skillets. "Sophie will *kill* us, smoking inside," Alistair said. Then he inhaled like a puffer fish and let an enormous blue cloud flow out.

I laughed. "Where is Sophie?"

Alistair shrugged, pouring the food on to three plates. "Out walking, I guess." He placed the skillets back on the stove, turned off the gas jets, and picked up his plate. "Bloody hell, I wish the airport would open."

"I hear ya, bro."

"Here, eat, you son of a bitch." Alistair shoved a plate to me. We walked to the living room to sit in front of the fire and ate together.

"This is good," I said with my mouth full. "This is the first thing I've eaten that isn't pizza." I swallowed hard, the big bolus of food easing down my gullet like a whole melon down a giraffe's throat.

"You inhaled it," Alistair said, chewing and smoking. "Did you use your teeth at all?"

"Nope, I'm saving them for the thaw." I belched. "Think Sophie wants her food?" Without waiting for an answer, I got her plate from the kitchen and shoveled the cold eggs, limp bacon, and congealing potatoes into my mouth. "I just need a biscuit for a napkin and I would be all right."

Sophie entered, regarding us balefully. "Well, I've seen power trucks and they're working, but there's so much damage and the ice keeps coming and so many outages, they're not even giving an estimate anymore of when we might get turned on."

"I'm turned on right now," I said, stretching my legs onto the coffee table and yawning luxuriously.

"Breakfast?" Alistair extinguished the tiny roach in his own leftovers and then held out the empty plate of cold grease I had cleared of food.

"Nice. Exactly what I wanted. Where is it?"

"Right here." I patted my belly.

"No, thanks, I'm good." Sophie unwound her muffler, unzipped her coat, and sat in the wingback across from us. "You know the trucks are coming from all over? I met some guys from North Carolina. North Carolina!"

"You previously mentioned that," Alistair said.

"Did I?" Sophie played with her coat zipper. "What about a generator? I'm about to cave."

Alistair and I looked at each other with our mouths open. Then we snapped into overdrive as if splashed with a bucket of Three Stooges water. Our voices overlapped in our giddy eagerness. "Sure…hell, yeah…whatever you wish…right away…absolutely." I didn't know about Alistair, but I was starved for television, Internet, something electric. But staying at Sophie's house, I endured the torture of her resistance to the horrid noise and hassle of a generator.

I worked every day to keep myself in a lather respecting Sophie's wishes. "No question it's the wisest decision…we just want you to be comfortable…" Our voices blended into an obsequious babble. We jumped up, bumped into each other, hit heads as we bent down to grab hats, tripped over each other getting our coats.

"Don't worry. We will go right now, won't we?"

"We will see to everything. You just relax." I picked up my gloves and Sophie's keys and dropped them. Alistair put his hat on backward. We stumbled out the door and into the car where we finally calmed.

"Suppose they're sold out. That would be a fine muddle, wouldn't it?" Alistair asked.

"Suppose nothing. It's guaranteed they're sold out," I said.

"Still, we can make the attempt." Alistair started the car.

"It's the least we can do," I added.

Alistair pulled into the street and nearly hit a pedestrian. Then he overcorrected and bumped the car up onto the curb. I got out and pushed while he spun the wheels. Finally, after me screaming myself crimson and pounding the hood, I freed the car by rocking it. Alistair drove away without me, yelling out the window, "I can't lose this momentum!" which is, of course, what happened several seconds later when he skidded the car into a crusty ice bank where it stuck. I walked up to the driver's side, expecting to have to yell my way into driving, but Alistair had already moved over.

When we arrived at the hardware store, it was just as busy as it had been that first panicky day. No generators.

"Damn and blast!" Alistair shouted, pounding a box. This was the most animated I had ever seen him.

"Goddamn it to hell," I moaned, sliding to the floor, my head in my hands.

"I can't take this anymore." We both said in unison.

A perky worker approached. "Crazy weather, huh? Need a generator?" We both stared at him like we were death row inmates. "We are out right now. They're selling so fast! Guess you should've gotten here sooner, ha, ha." He cleared his throat awkwardly. "We will have more in a few hours."

Alistair grabbed the boy by the collar. "When, you bloody sod, *when?*"

I stood up and separated them. "Easy," I told Alistair. Then I grabbed the back of the boy's neck. "He asked you when?" Alistair separated us.

The boy rubbed his neck. "In four hours. The truck is coming from Dallas."

"We'll wait, all right?" Alistair dropped like a stone to the concrete.

"Surely, sirs. If there's anything else you need, let me know." The worker sauntered away.

"What now?" I said.

"We wait, of course," Alistair said. "Why? Do you have to be elsewhere?"

I jumped to my feet. "Do you think they have phones here?" Alistair didn't answer so I wandered off in search of an emergency cell. Once I found a burner, I turned on the power and called Marny. Shreds of a dream were coming back to me.

"Hello?" Marny's voice was uncertain. She didn't recognize the number.

"It's Rogers."

"Electrified yet?"

"Not at the house, but about something else. What do you know about Perryman?"

"You mean *Sheriff* Perryman?"

"Who else? And what can we find out about this daughter-in-law, Wanda Perryman? She was fucking dismembered. That's so extreme, it has to be somebody close to her."

"I know, Jesus, Jim is so happy about this, he's practically prancing around the office. Perryman beat out a crony of his for the office of sheriff."

"Could it be a setup?"

"From my end? I doubt it. Jim's a pain in the ass, but I don't think he has the stomach for anything but political corruption," Marny said with finality.

"So Wanda's got some soft priors, but nothing that would result in a death like this," I said, thinking out loud.

"What about Wanda's husband?"

"Perryman's son?" I remembered him looking absolutely undone and seemingly ready to dissolve into sobbing. "Don't think so. His grief is real."

"Well, Wanda's priors are for drugs. What about a stiffed dealer or gangs or cartel?"

"Marny, you know dismemberment isn't their MO. They *want* their vics ID'd. Remember that crazy case last year when that amateur dealer was killed and the murderer spread the body in potted meat and left it in the forest?"

Marny laughed. "Yeah, that couldn't have been cheap. And even the carnivorous animals wouldn't go near that mess like they hoped they would."

"Yeah, even something like that isn't personal. Not like taking the time to saw off the head and hands and remove the teeth. Can you imagine the determination that takes?"

"I wish I couldn't, but I've been an ADA long enough that I can imagine it. Remember that guy who bit off his ex-girlfriend's nose?"

"Ew." I shuddered. I had testified for the prosecution in that one. "I will never forget. They even hoped to save her nose, but he had swallowed it and her nose was dissolved in the stomach acids before they could catch that perp."

"Yeah, poor thing had to come to court like that."

"Well, we nailed him, didn't we?" I said. "He got twenty years for GBH."

"I know. I tried to sell the jury on attempted murder, but it didn't work," Marny said wistfully.

"Well, I'm going to do some poking around Wanda's intimates. Call this number if you find anything on your end."

"Check."

When Alistair and I finally obtained the generator, it was so awkward and heavy that my new burner phone slipped out of my pocket and I accidentally stomped on it. When we got the generator loaded into Sophie's car, I ran back inside to buy another phone but they were all gone.

CHAPTER TWENTY-SEVEN

So how's work going then?" Alistair asked on our way back to Sophie's.

I sighed heavily. "Homicide is hard. And this weather makes it impossible," I said vaguely to deflect him. My murder muse was almost on to something. "How's your work?"

"Nearly finished. Watch it!" I hit what I thought was a large snowball, but was in fact, a small boulder. "So, really, what's happening these days?"

"Let me have your phone," I said. Alistair handed me his cell. "Shut up!" I pre-emptively ordered him, struggling to remember Perryman's number. I dialed. Wrong number. Shit. I tried again.

"Perryman," the sheriff answered hoarsely.

"Rogers. Did you run down any witnesses on Goodson?"

"Yeah, we have a few lukewarm sightings."

"Anybody pick him out of a six-pack?"

"Not yet, but we're about halfway through the list. One guy at a gas station said a guy matching Goodson's description bought gas and was, and I quote, a 'natural-born asshole' end quote."

"Okay, well we're definitely looking for one of those. Make Goodson take a polygraph."

"Don't be an ijit. Those aren't admissible in court," she said.

I rolled my eyes and pounded my fist on the steering wheel. Alistair reached over to correct our course. "*I know.* Just do it."

"It's a waste of time," Perryman said.

"I know that, you know that, but *he* doesn't know that. It doesn't matter what we think of polygraphs; all that matters is what Goodson thinks of them, and I guarantee that will scare him enough to break. Do it." I hung up and handed Alistair's cell back. "You were saying?" I said to him.

"Just asking about work. Anything juicy?"

I rubbed my chin. "I believe so."

"Ever have any serial killers in Tulsa?"

Alistair even made the words "serial killer" sound elegant. "Serial killah," I said, aping him and feeling foolish. I cleared my throat. "Yes, actually, we have. The rumor is that Ted Bundy is even responsible for a few unsolved murders here."

"Really?"

"Yes, on his way to Florida forty-odd years ago, it was alleged he stopped awhile here. But that was back when the earth was still cooling. We don't have any evidence. We can't prove it."

"Ted Bundy...flippin' heck. I'll be gobsmacked."

"Funny thing about serials...many of them are necrophiliacs also," I said.

Alistair blinked rapidly. "And that's funny?"

"No." I laughed. "The *funny* thing is, that the taboo against necrophilia is so deep that even a serial killer won't cop to it. They'll freely admit, even boast about the numbers of murders and how they were done. But necrophilia? That's the line they draw."

Alistair shuddered. "That's not so much funny as...profoundly upsetting."

"Tomayto tomahto," I said.

CHAPTER TWENTY-EIGHT

W e got it!" I hollered into the house to Sophie.
"Where the fuck have you been?" Sophie said. "I'm
not sure which one of you to hit!"

Alistair and I pointed at each other simultaneously and said,
"Her" and "him" in unison. Then Alistair said dryly, "You're
welcome," then added, "Aren't you chuffed? We put that beast on the
south side of the house where it would be most sheltered. Now we
just need to decide what to plug in." He rubbed his hands together.

"Refrigerator," Sophie said.

"TV," I said.

"Computer," Alistair said.

"Vacuum," Sophie said, looking around, "and lamps."

Alistair and I went outside, filled the generator with fuel,
negotiated with extension cords, appliances, windows that were
frozen shut, and a nervous, fluttery, bossy Sophie so overbearing
that Alistair ordered her into a hot bath or he would tranquilize her
with an elephant dart. Finally, we started the engine.

"Sweet!" I screamed over the noise.

"Let's go inside!" Alistair screamed back.

We studied the manual, did the power math, and first plugged
in the refrigerator and the vacuum. We agreed the least we could do
would be to clean up. Alistair put a trash can by the refrigerator and
began sniffing and discarding things. I picked up the living room

and then ran the vacuum. After that, we plugged in the television, computer, and two lamps. I turned the gas fireplace on high and then checked on the local news.

Alistair sat on the couch in a half-lotus with his laptop perched on his legs. He was humming.

"Pretty nice, huh?" I gestured to the clean room and the power. Alistair didn't respond, his gleeful hum like happily darting magpies.

Sophie emerged, looking fresh and pink. The bathrobe she had on was so large and thick, I could only see her eyes and forehead. "Very nice," she said, smiling for the first time in days. "Thank you."

"You're welcome." I approached and embraced her.

"We can't...Alistair." Sophie said, stiffening in my arms. I parted the edges of her robe like flower petals. The warm, clean fragrance that rose off her skin intoxicated me. I traced my fingertip from her breastbone to her collarbone to her throat to her chin. "He is in cyberspace. He wouldn't notice now if we buggered the Queen right here." I tilted her chin and lowered my mouth to hers. Her mouth met mine eagerly. There were no fireworks. Instead, it was a passion so languid, it was like thick syrup filling our veins, rising sweetly, slowly, like sap, making every muscle turgid with desire. It was a lazy river of lust, and we floated, too drugged on bliss to have any urgency. I pulled away and blinked my eyes like a sleepy lizard in the sun. Sophie had the secret smile of a sloth. We clasped hands and let go. That's all the agreement we needed. I caressed Sophie's shell pink cheek. "Alistair? I'm going to make love to Sophie tonight." My eyes never left her face.

Humming. Keyboard clicks.

"I'm going to pleasure her until she begs for mercy." I stroked Sophie's ear. She blushed, closed her robe, and tightened it again and walked to the bedroom. "See you in a minute!" I called, dancing on euphoric bubbles.

"No, you won't, not yet!" Sophie answered and I heard her deadbolt the door.

"Aw, fuck!" I said to Alistair. "Can you believe that shit?"

Keyboard clicks. Tuneless humming.

"You're a zombie and she still wants to wait! I cannot survive these blue balls!" I cupped my crotch and flopped on the couch with the TV remote.

"Jill? You say something, mate?" Alistair looked genuinely surprised.

"Not a word," I said, changing channels. There was nothing on but dire weather predictions and reality shows. I found a channel on which a local news anchor was announcing that Rick Goodson was being released and no charges would be filed. Rage replaced desire instantly. I automatically fumbled for my phone to call the chief before I remembered. "Goddammit! Goddammit!" I jabbed Alistair with my elbow. "Does Sophie have a land line?"

"What makes you think I would know? Ask her."

I stormed to Sophie's bedroom door and pounded on it.

"Who is it?" Sophie called sweetly.

"Your future," I said.

"I can't open the door. I want to be surprised."

"Oh, you will be! I need a land line. You have one hidden somewhere?"

"Why don't you go home already?"

"Why don't you put out already?"

"Good one," Sophie said sarcastically. "Just a minute." When she opened the door, she was still wrapped in the robe that was as large as a comforter. She turned on a flashlight and went to another room to search for a phone. I didn't follow because I didn't trust myself and didn't need any more misery. Sophie returned with a beige push button desk model phone. She went to the living room, plugged the cord into the wall, and set the phone on the side table.

"How old is this thing?" I asked.

"Really? And where's your phone?"

I sat down, picked up the handset, punched in the numbers, and waited. "This phone is dead!" I said, slamming it down so hard the bell chimed.

Sophie and Alistair both burst out laughing. "What did you expect, Jill? That I have land line service on tap? Would you like to send a telegram? How about a fax?"

"Fuck you both. And the horses you rode in on."

"Leave the horses out of this," Alistair said.

"Anything else, Jill?" Sophie asked. Without waiting for my reply, she said, "Excellent. Good night."

"I'm going for a walk," I said to Alistair.

"Mind your knickers, won't you?" Alistair said as I closed the front door behind me.

"I'm trapped in hell," I said to myself. "Something's got to give."

The icy black night was so quiet, it pressed on my eardrums. The darkness was deep, palpable, and ominous without porch lights, streetlights, city lights, and traffic. Suddenly, I didn't want to move off the porch. What had seemed like hell a few seconds ago now seemed like heaven with lights and a fire and shelter from this brutal weather. I didn't know what to do, but sleeping seemed like a good solution.

"Back already?" Alistair asked as I stood with my back to the roaring fire.

"It's cold," I answered.

Alistair regarded me over reading glasses that had slid down his regal nose. "That's one thing about you Americans. A firm grasp on the obvious."

"Don't start," I groaned. "Make me a sandwich."

Alistair laughed and began typing again.

"Worth a shot," I said. I wrapped a thick comforter around myself, beat a pillow into submission, and curled into the wingback.

Sophie shook me awake. "Jesus, Jill, your snoring is moving the furniture. Wake up."

"Sorry." I stretched and felt everything pop.

"Here, I went out for gas for the generator and picked up something for you." She handed me a cell phone.

"Hot damn!" I said. "I've got my life back!" I stood, grabbed her, and kissed her forehead. "Can I shower?"

"It's an order. Brush your teeth too," Sophie said. "Wait for Alistair to finish. Want some breakfast? We can have toast now."

"No, just some coffee. We can have actual brewed coffee now, right? Not just that instant powder shit?"

"Ground the beans myself not an hour ago."

I dashed into the kitchen realizing for the first time how much I had missed the smell and even the sound of coffee. Without it, the air seemed dull and depressing, the hours a long trudge to a dead end, but that fragrance meant everything was okay. The day would be orderly and successful and pleasurable. Coffee completed the morning and filled in everything that was missing.

I searched the cabinets until I found the largest tanker I could and poured the coffee pot's entire contents into it. I found sugar and poured that in until I saw the fluid rise an inch. Then I stirred and tasted. Perfect.

"Cream?" Sophie asked, offering a carton from the fridge.

"That's right! We can have dairy now." I took the cream and poured until the coffee turned the color of Penelope's skin.

"I have a paint bucket that is larger than that if you'd prefer," Sophie said, raising an eyebrow at my huge mug.

"No, I think sixty-four ounces will be just fine for my first serving." I gulped the scalding liquid. I sighed happily. "This makes everything better. I just need some cigarettes. How's the weather?" I asked, thinking that I would have to go out for tobacco and supplies.

"It's actually thirty degrees today, so if the sun comes out, the ice will start melting."

I grinned, feeling as fine as a plump puppy. "I'm gonna call the chief; I'm gonna do some heavy brainstorming in the bathroom on Perryman; I'm gonna rent a car; I'm gonna get tobacco, and then I'm gonna call Penelope."

Sophie stared at me through half lids, her eyes as flat as dull pennies. "Then you need to go home."

"I'm not like you. I can't go all year without the good thing. I'm no sexual camel."

"Fine. Give me that coffee and get out." Sophie took my mug before I could register what was happening. She held the cup high over her head and poured the coffee down the sink in a dramatic arc.

"What...?" I stared disbelievingly at my empty hands, my mouth still tingling with the leftover flavor of my perfect coffee.

"Are you just about stupid?" Sophie said and stormed from the room.

I shrugged and began grinding beans for a fresh pot. Sophie reappeared in the doorway, leaning against the jamb. Anger sizzled and snapped off her skin and hair, but she was dead calm. She pointed at the coffee maker with her chin. "I wouldn't."

I stopped. "Then what? You want me to marry you for coffee?"

"Get over yourself. Just go home. You can have all the coffee and hussy pussy you want."

"I can't have *you,*" I said.

"Not yet."

"No," I cried. "No! I can't live on hope and promises. I won't pledge myself to you for nothing. Either we are together and all that means or we are not."

"You are positively puerile."

"You still want me." I turned to her and grinned, my hypnotic and undulating desire enveloping us both.

"Not like this. I've told you! Why can't you understand? Why can't you just be decent and let the airport open and Alistair go home? Do you really want to be that cruel?"

"Why can't he be decent and get a hotel near the airport? Why is he still here?"

"Really? *You're* still here." Sophie's eyes blazed. "I've dumped him and now you want me to kick him out in the ice storm? Is that who you are?"

"It's him or me."

"But Alistair and I are not together!" Sophie said.

"If you don't choose me now, you never will," I said, an icy chill invading my blood. "There will always be something in the way."

"Oh, come on!" Sophie said. "Be fair!"

"Be brave," I said coldly.

"I can't believe it. This is the line you want to draw?"

I crossed my arms and traced my toe along the floor between us.

"Be careful, Jill," Sophie whispered, her voice a plea. "What you do now cannot be undone." Sophie's cheeks were magenta with the effort not to cry.

My eyes glittered with tears too, but I was a solid iceberg. I don't know where this ultimatum came from, but I was sticking to it. Don't you know I'm in love with you? My collarbones cried. Don't you know I'm afraid of being hurt so I'm testing you? My arms insisted. Don't you know I'm sick of waiting and limbo? My hip bones murmured.

"Don't do this," Sophie said, tears tracing a straight stream down her face.

I blinked. I was far away and numb. I traced my toe on the invisible but fatal line once more. Sophie released an anguished cry and ran from the room.

I packed the few items I had into my parka pockets. I upended the empty coffee tanker into my mouth to catch any leftover drops, and I closed Sophie's front door behind me.

The sun was out and the top layer of ice was beginning to dissolve into slush. If I couldn't find a ride, I would hitchhike. I pressed Marny's number into the phone Sophie bought me and felt so guilty, I almost ran back and apologized. But my stubborn, proud streak decided just to pay Sophie for the phone.

I knocked on the door. When Sophie opened it, her face brightened. "Jill...I—"

"For the phone." I thrust some bills into her hand. She shook her head, her face breaking apart. She closed the door gently without speaking. The bills lay in wads on the icy walk. I left them. Finally, Marny answered my call.

"Come get me," I said, my voice sadder than I realized.

"Oh, bubby, be right there," Marny said. I sat on the curb and waited, feeling like I was drowning in regret. I kept gasping for air. I didn't know how to undo any of my foolish mess, and I was afraid to try.

CHAPTER TWENTY-NINE

A rusty dented minivan finally pulled up and stopped. "What the hell is this?" I opened the passenger door with a hard tug and a loud screech.

"My nephew's. Where to?"

"Penelope's."

Marny began driving. I closed my eyes to try to contain my pain. Why had I done that stupid standoff?

I was such a shit! Why would anyone care about me? But I had been lucky enough to nearly capture the heart of that incredible woman who had been generous enough to take me in, and I go cave man on her. I moaned, reliving that shameful scene. If only I could have another chance! I would swear to be good and wait as long as she wanted, and Alistair could live with us if he so desired. But I really screwed it up. I kept replaying the vision of Sophie's hopeful face when she opened the door and me, a knuckle-dragging Grade-A asshole shoving money at her. Sophie closing the door so quietly was an ominous sign of her resignation.

I had showed her the truth of my small selfish soul, and I would never be trusted again. She had even warned me! And what did I get for my stubbornness? Me—single, lonely, cold, heartbroken, and made even worse by the knowledge that this had been preventable, and it was entirely my fault. Oh, that burned like karmic acid. I opened my eyes to tell Marny to take me home instead of to Penelope's, and I saw that she had parked in front of Sophie's.

"Here we are!" Marny trilled.

My limbs were granite. "I can't go back there."

"Just put me out of my misery. I've never seen you like this over any quim. So go make up already. No amount of Penelopes can help you now."

"No."

Marny rolled down her window and awkwardly climbed out, her quilted ski pants hooking briefly on a piece of protruding metal. "Door won't open," she explained. "Either you're coming with or I'm going alone, but I can't take anymore of this twat opera!"

"I fell on my sword. It's too late."

"We'll see." Marny trudged up the steps. I checked the ignition. Damn! She took the keys so I couldn't drive. I curled into a ball of embarrassment and tried to will myself dead. In spite of the blinding sun and the sounds of ice dripping and crashing to the ground all over the neighborhood, a bone chill began invading me like a creeping exhaustion. I couldn't wait much longer. I would start walking and Marny could find me. As I began stretching to get out and take off, Marny and Sophie walked to the van. I tensed, automatically putting my hand on my holster and realizing what an idiotic thing that was, removed my hand, and just sat, jaws clenched. Zippo. Zippo. Zippo. Marny motioned for me to get out. I rolled my eyes, hit the door with my shoulder, and leaned against the van with my arms crossed and stared at my boots, finger flipping my Zip.

Marny clapped once. "Jill, I understand you've made an ass of yourself again and that you would like to make amends?" she asked sweetly.

Sophie, her face closed and wintry, just stared ice picks at me.

"Yes," I mumbled.

"Yes, what?" Marny prompted.

"Yes, I fucked up. Yes, I want to apologize." I answered, not daring to look at Sophie. Click open. Click closed. I fumbled my last cigarette out of the case, bit it, lit it, and puffed nervously.

"And, Sophie, are you willing to overlook this baboon behavior, be the bigger person yet again, and forgive this blockhead once more so we can all get on with our lives?"

Sophie paused. Time stretched into a sharp, thin wire. Ice slid off roofs and tree limbs and smashed to the ground in arctic explosions all around us. Otherwise, the city was dead quiet. I couldn't even hear Sophie's generator. I finished my cigarette, licked my thumb and forefinger, and pinched out the roach. I could feel the pulse of each passing second with my heartbeat. I couldn't stand this. "Fuck it!" I yelled. "Marny, get your ass in gear and take me home *now!*"

"Fine!" Sophie screamed, the veins bulging in her sweet stem of throat, "who needs you?"

"Okay," Marny said, "let's begin again. Jill, do you promise not to be a horse's ass for the next two…no, the next minute?"

I glanced at Sophie, who was almost smiling. "I do," I said.

"And, Sophie, do you promise to stand here for the next minute?"

"I do," Sophie said.

"Well, all right! Jill, please think about your words very carefully, not just twice but three times before you speak any aloud and tell Sophie what is going on."

I took a breath. "Sophie, I—"

"That's good, Jill. Stop there," Marny said. Sophie smirked. "Okay, Jill, ready?" Marny asked. "Keep going."

"Fine," I said. "Sophie, I—"

"Jill, I think it's time to remind you to speak carefully," Marny said.

I nodded. "Sophie—"

"Jill," Marny warned me, "easy. Kind. Like you're speaking to a newborn. Or a preacher. Or a newborn preacher."

I drew my finger across my throat at Marny. Sophie, arms locked over her body, full of amused skepticism, waited. A tree limb fell to the ground, making all of us jump. What should I say? Should I explain my fears? Be casual? Cool? Rational? Lie and blame it on hormones? Blame it on my job? Beg? Or a straight up apology? I had to be cool. I couldn't be naked and vulnerable out here, in front of Marny.

"Sophie," I began again.

"Newborn preacher," Marny said.

I stood in front of that glorious woman and raised my arms and shoulders in a shrug. Sophie lifted her eyebrows, her mouth puckering. Sophie began to turn away, and I dropped to the ice in desperate supplication. My trousers were soaked immediately. The cold wetness felt good on my nervous, overheated knees. "I'm in love with you! You're the only woman I've ever loved and you're all I want. I'm scared and difficult and frequently a jerk!" I shouted.

"Creep," Marny added.

"Creep too," I said. "I am so crazy about you, it makes me cuckoo. If I weren't completely sprung, all this would be easy. But it's serious, so I sabotage it," I called to Sophie's back, "and I might not be worth it!"

"Good! Good, Jill!" Marny said. "Sophie, I don't know you well, but I do know this. You are *way* out of Jill's league. You are not even on the same planet. In her finest dreams, she is nowhere close to being good enough for you."

Sophie's back thought about things. Marny and I waited, exchanging glances. "Come inside," Sophie finally said, starting to walk to the house again.

"Oh, yeah!" I crowed. "Gotcha right here." I wiggled my pinkie as I stood up in triumph.

Marny kicked me in the shin. "Jill, no! Bad, Jill, bad!" Sophie just kept walking. "You make this work!" Marny said through clenched teeth. "Because I'm not coming over here again."

I limped after Sophie. "I'm in!" I gloated. "You can go."

"Good. I have a…" Marny paused meaningfully, "houseguest. Friend of the family."

"I'm one of those too." I grinned, licking my lips. Marny rolled her eyes. "Oh, Jill, I'll call you in fifteen minutes to see if you need a ride home."

I waved her off and followed Sophie back into paradise.

CHAPTER THIRTY

I walked through the front door to find Alistair engrossed in his computer again. "Bedroom," he said to me. I blinked in surprise but followed the hallway to the master.

There, on top of all the comforters was Sophie, nude. My eyes bulged, my mouth flooded with moisture, and my heart trip-hammered. I became humble and insecure at the glowing magnificence of her skin. I had stopped in shock at the doorway. I was being ungallant because she must have been freezing, but I was struck dumb and immobile. "Are you sure?" I whispered, beginning to tremble.

"For God's sake, how many signals, hints, and clues do you need? Do you ever hook up?" Sophie slid her legs open in a snow angel arc.

In my mind, I was sprinting over and leaping on top of her like a ravenous bear onto a plump salmon. But I was stuck. I had lead foot. My voice would merely click.

"Jill?" Sophie sat up and gathered pillows and blankets over her.

That broke the spell. "Sophie," I said. I felt Marny's rolled up newspaper, swatting my nose in warning. "Sophie...it's too much pressure." I felt my internal tide switch abruptly to stormy high seas, and I choked on a sob. I fled down the hallway to the warm living room with the crackling fire and sweet lamplight. I collapsed on the couch, shaking and gasping, willing back tears. I hung my head and tried to calm down.

"Did the earth move?" Alistair said.

"I lost it, man," I said simply.

Alistair turned to me and shrugged. "She does have that effect, doesn't she? Keep trying. It's rather like riding a bicycle."

"Have you ever ridden a bike?"

Alistair laughed and continued typing. "Can't say that I have, actually."

"Well, she's the Tour de France, and I don't feel like a champ."

"Come on, sport. You're Les Armstrong," Alistair said.

"Lance. Lance Armstrong," I corrected him.

"Oh? Right you are then. Keep your pecker up. Off you go."

I stood up and returned to the bedroom. Sophie was lying on her side, her back to me, buried in blankets. I sat on the bed. I felt Marny rubbing my nose in my mess.

"Sophie, I'm sorry," I said, tears clotting my voice. I cleared my throat several times.

She rolled over and smiled. "It's okay. It is a big deal."

I exhaled, relieved, all my joints loosening.

Sophie lifted the edge of the comforter and motioned invitingly. "It's warmer in here."

"Okay, but no funny stuff." I began removing my clothes but felt bashful. "Turn your head."

"Lock the door."

At last, I was nestled in bed. Sophie and I didn't touch. I lay stiffly and stared at the ceiling. I reflected on how easy it had been with all those other women. Effortless. Like riding a bike. I laughed.

"What?" Sophie asked.

"Something Alistair said."

"He gave you some tips?"

"As a matter of fact, yes." I rolled to face her. "Why don't we just start with..." I slid my hand to hers and knit our fingers, "this?"

Sophie looked scared too. "Okay." Then she giggled. "I've never been so nervous. Not even my first time."

"We're not doing anything. Just this." I stroked her hand for emphasis.

"Yes," Sophie said, nodding. "Just this."

We lay in bed, our hands curled together like timid baby bunnies. Our breath became synchronized. We blinked and smiled in unison. The sun was obliterated by clouds, and the room grew dim and gray. Soon, we heard the ominous tick of raining beads.

"Ice again," Sophie said happily.

"Don't care," I said, trying to completely absorb all the beautiful complexity of Sophie's face.

"Streets will be even worse now that it's melted some," she added.

"Good. Power crews have no hope of finishing soon."

"Comme il faut," she said.

I didn't ask what that meant. We closed our eyes and slept simultaneously, drifting sweetly in our bed island, needing only each other's heartbeat to feel completely content and nourished.

The room was the color of twilight when we both opened our eyes. Our hands were still joined, and Sophie had such a look of luminous peace that I had to cough into my pillow not to cry. I might be unfit for the force if I continue to fall in love, I thought. So what? It's worth it, came the immediate response. "I love you," I whispered hoarsely, to my own surprise.

Sophie smiled. "I know you do. God help me, I love you too. I've tried not to, God knows I have, but I can't help it, and there's nothing I can do about it." Then she rolled on top of me, her silken skin caressing and fitting mine as if a satin sheet had been fluffed, shaken, raised, snapped, and allowed to float down to cover me. At the jolt of pleasure, I stiffened. Sophie rolled her eyes. "What's wrong now?"

"We should wait. To be sensitive to Alistair and all." Suddenly, I understood how painful it must be to try to live without Sophie. To have had her touch and her smile and then to try to get on with life without her…impossible. Excruciating. My heart broke for Alistair, sitting alone in the living room.

"No, Jill, he's a grown-up. He's fine. Believe me; this will solve all our problems."

"What if you're wrong?" I said, turning my head to avoid her kiss.

"Let's find out." Sophie's mouth on my ear, my neck, and then my shoulder, was so convincing that I almost agreed.

"Man or woman, I've never had to work for this," Sophie said.

"I'm trying to—" I gasped, clutching the mattress and sheets, "be a better person!"

"Do that on your own time. Right now, you're mine." Sophie sat up and straddled my chest. Any scrap of sense I had left was obliterated by the sight of her slow undulation over me. She leaned all the way back onto my legs and opened her knees wider. I struggled to get loose, but I was pinned good.

I was finally able to get one hand free, and I stroked her thigh. She moaned, and like a pebble dropped into a sweet, still pond, at my touch, her skin rippled with goose bumps. Sophie took my hand and caressed her cunt with it.

"Know me," she whispered. She raised her other knee for me to have my trapped hand loose, and I cupped her buttocks and pulled her closer.

"Know me," she repeated.

"I am starting with my eyes," I said. I gorged on the delicious sight of her. I loved that her pubic hair was a soft, cinnamon sugar brown in contrast with her riot of golden curls on her head. Her delicate, tan eyebrows, like butterfly antennae, were a preview to the secret, barely brown Venus hiding below. Then the juicy split in the center like a sliced pomegranate, bursting with ruby seeds, protected by fragrant folds of flesh. To know her, I had to weigh, measure, sniff, feel, taste, and memorize. Her right labial lip was slightly plumper than her left; her pubic hair was a mat of crazy curls in absolutely perfect corkscrews. She had a dark mole on her upper, inner left thigh. Her skin on either side of her mons was slightly abraded, from shaving or waxing. She had a simple, fresh, clean smell like pineapples in the sun.

The hair on her thighs was so fine and white, it was nearly invisible. Her navel was a perfect cup. I longed to drop an orchid into it. Her skin was rosy with a sandy undertone, like milky cocoa and blush roses. She had a few stretch marks on each hip, white zigzags in her peachy, caramel skin. From a teenaged growth spurt, I assumed. Her breathing was deep and steady but with an intense ragged edge of passion. I found a cayenne sprinkling of freckles on the top of one turgid leg muscle. I arched my neck and kissed the inside of her thigh. She groaned. I tasted electricity and very faintly, salt. I suckled and bit. Sophie gyrated as well as she could in her awkward position.

"Calm down," I said to her throbbing skin. "It takes a long time to know you."

A low laugh gurgled from her throat, and she was still.

I ran my fingertips lightly over her skin, which rose in a glissando of pleasure.

"You don't have to restrain me," I said, finding her hands and pulling her upright. We embraced. My face was happily smothered by her breasts. But this was too important to rush. So instead of biting a hole to her heart, smearing myself in her hot, tribal blood like ownership paint, throwing Sophie onto her back and ravishing her so hard that she would be permanently crippled, I gently stroked her breasts. My touch and her skin were both so soft that where I ended and she began was indiscernible. I slowly moved to place Sophie on her back. She watched me, unblinking. I unfolded her legs and placed them chastely together. Then I wrestled part of the comforter to cover all but her feet.

"I will start here," I said. Sophie stretched and wiggled her toes in response. I caressed her feet, studying every detail. They were bony, long and thin. The longer I stared at them, the more they resembled an alien flipper. Her soles were hard like leather, and the tops of her feet were crisscrossed with bulging veins like a 3D topography map. I had never seen so many veins and capillaries in one place! I looked at my own feet briefly. Smooth and square, dull and boring. But Sophie's feet—I could trace the path of blood from her calf, down and around her ankle, curling into her arches, fanning out to her toes. I pressed on a blue-green vein and then watched, fascinated, as the color drained from the vein where I held it and then returned, quick as lightning, when I released it. "Can you feel that?" I asked.

"Your finger on my foot?"

"No, the blood stopping and starting."

"No, are you playing?"

I laughed. "A little. I'm learning you." I stroked the deep hollows between the bones that led to the toes. They were as prominent and taut as harp strings. As if her toes were marionettes secured by these lines. Her toes were tiny, almost inconsequential, as if they belonged to another foot entirely. They were thin with clearly outlined joints and small, perfect nails. I rubbed each of them to discover the miniature bones within. I dug my knuckle into her sole to feel the toothsome meat. Then, I breathed on her toes. Sophie moaned, her eyes closed. I licked very deliberately in between each toe before engulfing her big toe in my mouth, causing Sophie to gasp and spasm. I sucked. I raked with my teeth. I bit and licked. I tasted river bed. I tickled the smooth river rock of her toe with my tongue. I sucked all ten toes this way, letting my mouth memorize their bends and curves. I only switched when I saw that she was trembling with desire. I placed pillows over her feet to keep them warm. I put my thick socks and parka back on, but was otherwise naked.

Sophie's calves! Small, compact, neat. Like little packs of dynamite on her legs, the muscles were dense and dangerous. Sophie's shin was as long and sharp as a razor; the bone felt barely sheathed in skin. I expected it to cut through any second and slice my hands. Her ankles were round like pulleys and her knees were smooth demi-spheres like oak knobs. I grabbed a fistful of muscle and kneaded it. Sophie groaned. I stroked her legs hard and enjoyed the rough stubble from her ankle all the way up to her knee on both legs. Her skin was chafed and rosy when I moved on to her thighs.

As I rearranged blankets, I noticed that Sophie was laid out and dopey as if I had poured her onto that spot.

I kissed her mouth and felt tension gathering. I cupped Sophie's cunt and felt her slick and swollen. She pressed against my hand. I left her mouth and bent over her turgid clit.

"Please," she whispered.

"Just for a second," I said. I licked the seawater from her pulsing cunt. Sophie cried out and began gyrating. I poised my finger right at her liquid center. How beautifully her cunt shone—full of life and lust.

"Oh, my God, Jill, please, please, please. I've never wanted anyone so much. I can't stand it. Please, please, please."

"Yes, Sophie, yes." I nuzzled her clit and drew it gently into my mouth. I was going to build this orgasm gradually. Stoke by stroke. No hurry. Sophie would come so hard and long, they would hear her at police headquarters downtown.

"Just relax. Let go. I'll take you there," I said to Sophie, whose arms and legs had begun thrashing.

"Fuck me!" she screamed.

"I will. Let it happen," I said, sliding two of my fingers deep into her.

"Ohhh," Sophie moaned ecstatically. I removed my fingers and sucked off the delicious glaze. "No!" Sophie yelled.

"I'm not finished knowing you yet," I said smoothly. I caressed her clit.

"Yes, yes, yes." Sophie's eyes rolled back and she spread herself so wide, I thought she would split in two. The blankets and pillows were thrown to the floor. Her pelvis rose in supplication. "Love me, Jill," she begged, "I need you."

"I am loving you, Sophie. You need to enjoy all of it," I said with determined calm. "Let me finish." I tickled and teased her twat. Sophie agreed, her limbs going limp. "I believe I was here." I sat between Sophie's thighs.

Suddenly, there was pounding on the bedroom door. "Jill! Jill!" Alistair called. "Wake up!"

"How polite of him to pretend we're sleeping," I said wryly. "Yeah?" I called, my voice gruff.

"Some sort of emergency!"

"Be right there."

Sophie murdered me with her glare as I stood and covered her with the comforter again. I had never seen eyes so black with fury. I put on my pants, shrugging.

"What can I do?" I asked, loving the taste of her on my lips.

Sophie said nothing, her eyes following me like a heat-seeking missile intent on my death.

"I can never resist you when you're so cute!" I cried. I climbed under the covers again and found Sophie's aching, dripping cunt. I pulled her thighs apart and breathed in her salty, fruity, tangy fragrance. I plunged my tongue into her slippery honey. Sophie cooed and wiggled, but then she gave me the shoulder tap and closed her legs, knocking me aside.

"Jill, it's an emergency. Go."

"The sheriff is probably just out of donuts," I said, still under the comforter, my voice muffled by the blanket. "Come on. Let me in." I wedged my hand in between her legs and felt that succulent sizzle.

"No, Jill, go ahead; I'll be here."

"Baby! Don't do this to me!" I rolled her on her belly and began biting and licking her buttocks.

"Ohhh, gawwwd," Sophie groaned, her legs loosening. I thrust into her cunt from behind and felt it clench to grip me. "Yes, yes, Jill, yes. Do it now. Fuck me forever!"

I caressed her clit with my other hand and kept a steady, firm rhythm inside her.

"Oh, God, oh, God…" Sophie began bucking.

"Jill, mate, you there?" Alistair shouting, banging on the door.

"That's it; we're done." Sophie curled into a cold comma and buried herself in blankets.

"Listen, I wouldn't wake you if it weren't an emergency," Alistair said.

"I know. I'm coming," I answered, shoving my feet into my boots.

"Well, you're the only one," Sophie said from the blankets.

"Shut up. You think I planned this?" I said harshly. Marny shook her finger at me. "I mean, I'm sorry, Sophie. Truly. I will make it up to you. Please forgive me. I don't want to go."

"I know," Sophie said from underneath a pillow. "Just hurry back."

"Like you won't believe!" I said, finding her face and kissing her.

As I walked away toward the door, I heard Sophie's cries building to a crescendo emanating from the comforter cocoon. Her sounds of delight infuriated me. "Like hell!" I screamed, diving into the bed. I tore the blankets off and uncovered Sophie with a blue dildo buried to its base in her muff. She was working it like a stripper on payday. I snatched it from her snatch. "If I can't; you can't," I seethed. Sophie shrugged. I threw the covers back over her and stumbled away when I heard the click and hum of a vibrator.

"Jesus, Mary, and Joseph, fuck all!" I yelled, reaching into the blankets to see Sophie splayed out, receiving service from a Magic Wand. Her cunt was pumping and she was panting, delirious moans pulsing from her throat. I yanked the plug from the wall. This time, Sophie attacked me like a tigress. She clawed my face and kicked my stomach, trying to get the toys back.

"No," I ordered, fending off blows. "No. Down, girl." I wrapped the dildo and vibrator together in the cord. "I'll just keep these."

Sophie grinned maliciously and wiggled her fingers in my face. "I still have these!" She said triumphantly.

I saw red. I dropped the toys, pinned Sophie to the bed, and secured her hands to the bedposts with zip ties from my belt. I was shaking with intensity. "No means no," I said. "That is mine." Watching her squirm seductively, I needed release or I would die. I felt my heart actually skip a beat. The pulse in my clit was like a kettle drum. "Okay, just once," I choked out. I raised Sophie's legs and parted them. I spread her puffy lips apart and placed my mouth on her cunt. My fingers slid home.

"Yes, finally, yes…" Sophie wept, jerking on the restraints.

"Yes, baby, yes, my love," I told her stiff clit.

"I'm coming!" Sophie cried joyously, falling apart like tender meat off the bone.

"Come on me! Give me everything," I answered.

"Jill!" Alistair thundered from the other side of the door. "I know this is a bit awkward, but you have a visitor. Please attend this instant!"

"Don't. Do. It. Stay. Just for a second. Don't. Go." Sophie grunted and squeezed her cunt around my hand.

Reluctantly, I rose. "I'll be back before you know I'm gone," I said. Because I knew Sophie was sly and crafty, I picked up the toys and covered Sophie again.

"Bloody hell, Jill, come on!" Alistair pounded the door.

"Fuck you, whaaaat?" I yelled, flinging open the door. I stood there shirtless, wearing only parka, pants, and boots with the toys dangling from my hand.

Sophie began screaming obscenities from the bed. "You no good son of a bitching tease! You sorry sack a shit! Get back here this minute! I will cut your balls off if you walk out that door! Don't you dare leave me like this! I'll fire your pig-cop ass. Just you try me!"

In the hallway with Alistair, stood Chief St. John.

CHAPTER THIRTY-ONE

O h, hi, Chief!" I said loudly enough for Sophie to hear. "Were you in the hood?"

"Fuck the chief! Fuck you, Jill! Fuck me, somebody fuck me now!" Sophie kicked and twisted.

"Sweet girl," Chief said. "Did I interrupt something?"

"She's an old friend of the family."

"You better hope the chief puts out because I never will again! You won't get another whiff of this!" Sophie screamed. Alistair, to my surprise, was blushing hard. He ran to the bed to try to soothe Sophie.

"I'm sorry to bust up your family reunion, but we have a situ," Chief said placidly.

"Sure, Chief, sure." I handed the toys to Alistair, who was perched on the edge of the bed. I picked up my shirt and followed the chief to the living room. "Sit down," I said and sat on the couch. I took off my parka. I was not embarrassed to be undressed in front of the chief. He had known me since I was a polliwog and he was family. I put on my soggy undershirt, then my shirt, buttoning and tucking it in. Then I buckled my belt and tied my bootlaces.

"Want to wash your hands?" Chief asked with a smile.

I looked at them. "Why?"

"Well, thank you for talking to me tonight. I know we both had other plans—"

A high-pitched scream came from the bedroom, and there was a crash and the sound of scrabbling like a dog trying to find purchase on a slick floor. "Good Lord!" Alistair appeared in the doorway, disheveled. "I need tea." He smoothed his hair, straightened his shirt, checked his pants, and stood up straight. "Anyone else?"

"No, thanks," we said in unison.

"What's up?" I patted my pockets for any remaining cigarettes even though I knew better. I wasn't a sloppy, absent-minded smoker who left cigarettes under couch cushions and half-smoked roaches in ashtrays everywhere. I was deliberate. I smoked one at a time and finished it completely, inhaling it all the way to ash before I started on another one.

"Goodson's gone. You and Dana scared the suspect bird off the nest."

I raised my chin and narrowed my eyes. "How do you know?"

"He's been under surveillance off and on; just keeping tabs, you know, and the next time Officer Dean checked the residence, it was vacant. He's gone for good."

"Kids and everything?"

"Yep. What do you have to say for yourself? You pressed him too hard."

"Oh, Chief, that's a steaming load. This is beneath you. You're looking for a fall guy when nobody but Perryman and I thought he was guilty of a crime. He was cocky and arrogant with us and pretty much guaranteed his own immunity because of his pal Jim Harrison."

"Jim says he's never heard of him."

"Jim says a lot of things to save his own fat ham."

"Well, what are you and Dana going to do now?"

"Um…I don't know, *look* for the sorry sack of shit?"

Chief looked at his watch. "When?"

"You need feet on the street this second? Sorry, not a minute before the thaw. I've already lost my car and phone. I am taking that as a sign from God."

Chief stared hopelessly out the dark windows. "That will be a while."

"Who's breathing down your neck about this?"

Alistair emerged from the kitchen with a giant mug. "Ah, yes, that's the stuff. Sure you don't want some tea and biscuits?" he asked us, taking a huge swallow from his big cup. "Mm, scalding. Just right."

"I've got to take off," Chief said, standing.

"So soon? You came over just for that? You banged me out of bed for this quickie?" I gesticulated in all directions, alarmed and confused.

"It's been a few days. I had to see your face. And you're obviously buried waist-deep here, so I had to come to you." Chief hardened his voice, "Is that all right?"

I shook my head, dispelling my disbelief. "Whatever. Good night."

"Visit's over already then?" Alistair put down his mug and walked the Chief to the door.

I called Perryman. No answer.

CHAPTER THIRTY-TWO

I ran eagerly back to the bedroom where I found Sophie dressed, sitting upright, working with her laptop, and talking on the phone. I started to remove my clothes, but she glared angrily at me and waved me out. I returned to the living room and stood by the fire, warming my perpetually chilled backside.

"You cut off Sophie's zip ties?" I asked Alistair who was typing on his laptop with one hand and hugging the mug to his chest with the other.

"I thought it was a bit extreme," Alistair said.

"Well, I'm the law in these parts, and extreme or not, this situation called for such measures to be taken." I surprised myself by sounding like an officious asshole. Why was I giving Alistair such a hard time? He was being nothing but gracious and helpful and a good sport about the breakup. In my head, Marny shook her head sadly and threw up her hands. Maybe I just couldn't eliminate that part of my personality entirely and it had to leak out somewhere. I was a cop, after all. Some say it's a prerequisite to have some strain of obnoxious prick in the character to make a successful officer.

Alistair looked at me with raised eyebrows as if he weren't disgusted by the maggot he now saw in front of him, but was merely puzzled and disappointed by it.

"Sorry, old chap. Got to disagree with you there," He said mildly. Then he returned to his computer and added, "I'm sure you have more plastic cuffies on you so if you do it again, I won't interfere."

"I'm sorry, Alistair. I don't know what gets into me." I prided myself in being able to admit. "Of course, you're right. Can we start over?"

Alistair smiled. "I insist. You're just a natural-born wanker, aren't you?"

I shrugged and clapped my hands on the outsides of my thighs. "Thank you." I shrugged again, trying to convey humility and sincerity. "Thank you for…just thank you."

Alistair's smile thinned. "Noblesse oblige? Pack it in."

"What the fuck is that? Whatever it is, it seems that I've pissed you off, so no, not that. I'm trying to reform and be nice. I'm such a wanker—"

Alistair held up a finger. "You can't say 'wanker' unless you've pledged fealty to the monarchy."

"Fine. I'm such a putz—" I waited for an objection and then continued, "I'm always saying the exact wrong thing and even I'm shocked by it. What I said before? I didn't mean a word of it. Just that Sophie and I were so close and the chief came by…" I rubbed my eyes, "and now, she's in there on her laptop and she's banished me."

Alistair laughed. "Sophie and her work. It's a sacred bond never violated by man or…" he appraised me, "beast."

"Good one," I said. "What's her job, exactly?"

"Oh, that is pathetic. You don't know what Sophie does for a living?"

I grinned. "You don't know either, do you?"

"Not a clue."

I dropped onto the couch, Zippo already weaving between my fingers and making its metal music opening and closing while exhaustion overtook me. "What do you *think* she does?"

"Well, she isn't an attorney or a chef, is she? That's all I've narrowed it down to thus far."

"You've never asked?"

"Frankly, I've always found Americans to be far too invasive. Within the first five, you want to know my job, age, marital status, number and ages of children, income, address, and immediate plans. It's a turn-off." Alistair finished his tea. "I left it to her to tell me if she wished and it never came up, so I left it alone. A free etiquette tip from the rest of the world to you nosy Americans. Enough already with the inquisition."

"But how else do you get to know someone?"

"Bloody hell! You think dry statistics bring you closer to someone's center? So you're ignorant and unimaginative as well, eh?"

"I'm a cop. That's how I'm built. To assess, find facts, measure, and evaluate."

"Give it a rest."

I laughed. "You want to say it, don't you?"

"Wanker."

"There it is."

"Just try to go a day without asking if someone is married. Just one day."

"I don't think I can quit cold turkey like that," I said, zipping up my coat.

"You will never let me down, will you?"

"I'll say it for you: wanker."

"You do realize that it isn't a compliment?"

"Der," I said, shrugging. "Doesn't bother me. It's kinda funny."

"So you're using it as a label so you can hide behind it and not change?"

"Wanker, ten-four." I pointed a finger gun at him. Alistair rolled his eyes. "There is no contempt on earth as sharp as that of an Englishman's affection," I said.

Alistair laughed. "True. Who said that?"

"Doy. I did."

"No, who *originally*?"

"Were you not listening? I did. Just now. Me."

"Jill!" Sophie called.

I stood, my bones popping and protesting. "My mistress beckons. I said that too."

"Ah, you're having me on."

"You think?" I slugged him on the shoulder and went to the bedroom.

CHAPTER THIRTY-THREE

Now maybe you'll put your trust in me and your faith in the Lord."

"But...how did...but...how?" I stammered.

"I won't gloat," Jim Harrison said smugly.

"What made you suspect anything?" I was slowly gathering the pieces of my mind together and putting on the worn, battered, threadbare cloak of accomplished homicide detective. I was not only surprised that I could be shocked after twelve years, but also keenly disappointed that it was this.

"We had done some routine investigation prior to the election to know exactly what we were dealing with."

I shook my head. The ice had stopped briefly. Jim and I sat in his Escalade, the modern equivalent of a Corvette for douchebags, but it did hold its own on the ice-packed streets. We were on an impromptu stakeout at Sheriff Dana Perryman's home.

I had returned to the bedroom to embrace Sophie only to be paged out of her arms by the DA. As much as I despised him, even more so since we were supposedly on the same side, I couldn't blow him off. He suggested we take a ride, and here I was, parked on the street, peering with binoculars through the woods. It was a full moon, made even brighter because it was encircled with ice crystals, like a thick ring of silver glitter.

Perryman's yard was luminous with moonlight. The dying bonfire in her side yard was clearly visible. I sighed. "What do you suspect exactly?" I massaged my forehead.

"At first, it was just the minor hints of possible misdemeanor drug associations."

"And now?"

"I leave the deductions to you, Detective." Jim's smile was like a Cheshire cat grimace in the dark.

"You gonna file charges?"

"Oh, again, I will let you handle that delicious task." Jim started the motor.

"Maybe she's just burning trash," I said, my murder muse knowing better. Trash burning was illegal so there was no legal reason to do it.

"Look at you," Jim sneered, gliding the vehicle forward down the street and away from the scene of my disappointment. "So high and mighty. So cocksure. So *certain,*" he hissed, "and now, just a gullible, mortal fool."

"Just because you're right about this doesn't mean you're right."

"Oh, Jill, Jill, Jill," Jim said sadly, "that's where you're wrong. Again. When will you learn that?" He patted my shoulder. I brushed him away as if his hand were a diseased tarantula. "Acceptance may come slowly for some, but it will come. Book of Harrison, verse 4:28."

"I prefer truth," I said.

"I am one and the same," Jim boomed. The car sped too fast on the icy highway.

"Don't talk to me like I'm one of your lackeys. I'm not on your payroll."

"You don't have to be on any payroll."

"Are you kidding me with this?" I cried. "How would that sound to the *Trib*? DA threatens detective?"

"I didn't threaten you." Jim's voice was clean and astonished.

I pulled the Glock from my shoulder and held it to his head.

"And neither did I," I said.

Jim snorted. "You have the safety on."

I cackled. "There's no safety on this one. The safety is right here." I used my free hand to point at my own head.

"Jill, don't do anything stupid."

"I know, you got there first," I said, my jaw clenched.

"What is this really about?" Jim asked, his voice hot and oily like mayo in the sun. "You want a raise? A promotion?"

"Let me out here. Now." I cocked the gun. Jim shrugged, pulled the vehicle to the emergency lane, and sped off as soon as my feet touched the ground.

I walked two miles back to Sophie's trying to sort it all out and find some peace.

CHAPTER THIRTY-FOUR

When I got there, Alistair was asleep on the couch and Sophie was waiting up in her giant cocoon robe. My skin was convulsively jumping like skittish, flyblown horseflesh, and my teeth were chattering hard. "Ikint sheel my hands and sheet" my teeth chopped the words.

"Your extremities are numb?" Sophie put me by the fire. "I'll run a tub." She disappeared. I stared longingly at the flames, debating about actually lying down in the center of the blaze. Every muscle in my body was in spasm with the effort of shivering. A giant clamp of tension had seized my neck. The only thing keeping me awake was my clownish teeth chattering ceaselessly.

Sophie returned and gently led me to the bathroom where the sunken tub steamed.

"I'm not taking my clothes off," I tried to say, but it came out like Ehm naht shakim cuzzoff.

"I know, baby. Just get in." Sophie lowered herself with me into the tub. She still wore her huge robe, which got soaked immediately like an enormous sponge.

The hot water was glorious. Like sweet air to a drowning person. I began to relax. My skin released and my muscles melted. My jaws stopped clicking. The clamp on my neck dissolved. I was overcome again with drowsiness.

"No, don't go to sleep." Sophie removed her robe, letting it sink to the bottom of the tub like a wounded ship. She floated on top of me. I grinned goofily. "Okay, you get sex started and I'll catch up."

She slapped me lightly. "Come on, wake up."

I kept my eyes closed, drifting dreamily in a womb of warmth. "I didn't take pills," I slurred drowsily. "You don't have to keep me awake."

Without warning, I felt a crash of frigid water hit my feet as Sophie turned on the cold tap. "You'll drown, dumbass. Get up."

She stood, pulled me to stand, and I knew I was in bad shape when I wanted sleep more than sex. I was like a somnolent child as she dried my body and dressed me in baggy flannel pajamas that had rocket ships all over them. "Don't ask," she said when I fingered the material. She wrapped herself in another robe cocoon and we walked to bed, which is the last thing I remember.

CHAPTER THIRTY-FIVE

When I woke up, Sophie was gone. Sunshine filled the room and made me giddy like helium, but it was still cold. I put on my parka and boots and went to the kitchen.

"Morning," I said to Sophie and Alistair. Sophie was stirring a pot on the stove and Alistair sat at the table with a newspaper. "What's different in here?" I sniffed. "Something's different."

"There are those legendary detective skills springing into action," Alistair said, reaching over to the switch plate on the wall and flicking it on and off. The light actually worked.

"Power?" I shrieked.

"That's it, splendid," Alistair said.

I poured a mug of coffee and sat at the table. "Where's the heat?"

"It's on," Sophie said, pouring the contents of the pot into two bowls. "It will take a while. Here." She set a bowl in front of me.

"And then hell came to breakfast. What is this slop?"

"Oatmeal. Eat it."

"I hate oatmeal."

"Everybody does, but believe me, you need it. I was under the covers with you," Sophie said.

"Very droll," I said, pushing the bowl away.

"Oh? I'll have it, shall I?" Alistair reached for the oatmeal.

"Forget it. You won't eat your way back into Sophie's bed." I stuck a spoon into the gluey, gelid mass and stirred.

"Oh, darn. And I was so hoping to." Alistair shook his newspaper indignantly.

"Alistair, have mine. I'll make more." Sophie smiled.

"Ta, love." Alistair smiled. He stirred brown sugar, raisins, cinnamon, and cream into the bowl and ate happily.

After seeing how much he was enjoying the glop, I copied him. Then I carefully raised a spoon of the mess to my mouth. "Mmm! Just like an oatmeal cookie." I paused and swallowed. "Hey, wait… it *is* an oatmeal cookie."

"I'll do the dishes. Why don't you get all shined up?" Sophie asked me. "You should probably check in with your office and your house."

"Ummm…okay…" I watched Sophie quizzically.

"She's sick of you already," Alistair said. "Must have been bloody awful flatulence."

"Are you?" I asked Sophie's back as she scrubbed the oatmeal pot.

"Of course not." She turned and wiped curls out of her eye with a sudsy forearm. "I just thought you would appreciate getting back out there…you know…keeping your life together, getting some work done."

"Oh, I'm working!" I exclaimed, cracking open the Zippo.

"Forget I said anything." Sophie turned back to the sink.

"I'm working, believe me!" I said.

"How?" Alistair asked, sipping fresh tea.

"Up here," I said, tapping my head. "I let my intuition percolate and then I just have to find the mistakes. And there are always mistakes."

"Rubbish." Alistair chortled.

"You're rubbish!" I said.

Sophie clanged the rinsed pot into the drainer and left the room.

"Here's what I figure," I said.

"Oh? What could that be?" Alistair replied.

"The daughter-in-law wasn't identified for *days*. She was booked into the morgue as a Jane Doe because she had no ID. Not only that, her hands and feet and head were cut off. When they finally found the hands and feet, the fingertips and toes were removed. And also, when they found the head in another part of town, the teeth had been pulled."

Alistair shuddered.

I began picking at a piece of cold, hard toast and tossing bits into my mouth, speaking aloud to myself. "See, she has some minor drug involvement, misdemeanor possession of controlled drugs, DUI, possession of marijuana, nothing fatal. But the line Dana got everybody to believe was that this Wanda chick was in deep with some mythical drug lord maniacs who assassinated her. Well, I call bullshit on that."

Alistair swallowed audibly, then sipped his tea and cleared his throat. "You do?"

"Yeah. There's no way some drug kingpin is going to bother with mutilating a body. They're in and out like the mob. Job done. And they *want* their vics ID'd because it sends a message to all the other rogue agents. No, no, no," I said, crunching toast loudly and clicking the Zippo.

"What then?"

"The more violent the offense, the closer the relationship between vic and perp. A drug hit would be a double tap. But this took care and time."

"A serial murderer?"

I pointed at Alistair. "Possible but unlikely. That's the sexy answer, but first we have to rule out the obvious."

"The husband."

"Usually, yes. But I'm looking at bigger game." My cell phone rang. "Hello?"

"Hi, lover. Come, come." Penelope.

Sophie entered the room and poured herself a cup of coffee. I coughed then said, "How did you get this number?" Marny, of course.

"A little bird told me your marriage might be on the rocks," she said.

Sophie's eyes blazed as she watched me fumble and fidget. Alistair smirked. I just hissed into the phone like a leaking tire and said, "Sorry, bad connection," And hung up. Zippo open. Zippo closed.

"Suave," Sophie remarked. "I didn't know Natives could blush."

"I can't do anything right for you, can I?" I bellowed at her. "I'm still here. I'm not at the office or I get called away when you do want me, or I fart or blink wrong. Fuck this!"

Sophie closed her eyes in resignation.

"Children, behave," Alistair said. "Jill, tell me more about this case."

"What are you doing?" I asked Alistair.

"He's trying to keep you from fucking up. Again," Sophie said, stirring sugar into her coffee at the counter.

"Is everything supposed to be my fault?" I said, louder than I intended. I saw a phantom Marny nodding emphatically in the doorway. I stood and approached Sophie. "Woman, I am this close to slapping you flat."

"That's so sweet. Could you put that in a frilly card?"

"Don't push me," I warned.

Sophie whirled and shoved me so hard and fast, I was on the floor before I could react. Alistair laughed. Sophie stepped over me and I grabbed her leg. She shook me off, holding her coffee mug over me. "Don't or I might spill this and I hate to waste coffee." She left the room. Alistair's laugh tapered to snorts and he held out a hand to help me up.

I took his hand and said, "I'm too old for this shit." At Alistair's look, I defended myself. "Well, someone had to say it! It's in the cop handbook!" I gestured to the hallway, meaning the departed Sophie. "Do you think it's over?"

"Don't be daft. She's barmy over you. Now, tell me more about this case."

I poured an extra large coffee and opened and closed the refrigerator several times in succession. "I just love electricity!" I finally got the cream, poured it empty into my coffee, and sat down. "Well, whatcha want to know?"

"What you're going to do next?"

I took a long, searing swallow and sighed. "Try to speak to the husband and get an alibi from Perryman." I remembered the sheriff's guard dog protectiveness. "Alone."

"Where was she found?"

"Which part?"

"Um…er…the main."

"Some kids out sledding on the east side called in a mannequin sighting. Those are always body dumps."

"You don't say."

"Yep." I took another long swallow. "How many mannequins have you ever seen outside? I'm betting zero. I've never seen one anywhere but in a store. But the human mind is bizarre—all witnesses who call in a suspected corpse say they think it is a mannequin, without exception. You'd think there would be mannequins littering the landscape like cigarette butts and beer cans." I patted myself, looking for cigarettes. "Shit!"

"What?" Alistair asked.

"I really need a smoke and I don't have any."

"What's that?" He tilted his head at the counter behind me. There, next to the drying dishes, was a carton of Camels.

"Let the choir say amen!" I said, relief flooding me like oxygen. I sat at the table, opened the box, then slit open a pack with my fingernail and lit a cigarette. "You're a straight guy," I said to Alistair and then looked him over. "Straight-ish. Guys who rape or guys who rape and murder, what's up with the no condom thing?"

Alistair shook his head. "What?"

"Well, I'm assuming these squirt bags don't want to get caught, and the gold standard for irrefutable proof is DNA, but guys are such sleaze balls that even the threat of the death penalty won't make them rubber up. My whole career I've wondered about it. So I figure, it's a selfish guy thing. You're a guy. What's up with that?"

"You're an absolute peach to consult me on this," Alistair said. "But we Brits do always use condoms when we rape, so you'll have to ask one of the local slimy hicks."

"You're no help at all."

"Wasn't trying to be."

Chapter Thirty-six

Suddenly, there were several explosions. It was daylight, but the kitchen was briefly filled with silver light as if giant flashes had gone off. Alistair and I leaped to the window and saw a power pole crackling with fire. There was one more blast, and the house went dark.

"No!" We heard Sophie scream. She ran into the kitchen with her hair curled over a half dozen round brushes with the brush handles protruding like great, tribal bones. "Tell me this is a joke," she howled, her eyes were wild. "Tell me one of you is fucking with the breaker!"

Alistair and I looked at each other. "Sophie," I said gently.

"Fix it!" She screamed, her face going red and a vein in her forehead bulging. "Fix it, fix it, fix it, fix it!"

"We're on it," I reassured her. "We're doing everything possible. It won't be long."

"Okay," Sophie panted, her eyes darting between us. "I mean, it's no big deal. I just want this to be over, you know? But it's no problem. I'm fine; I'm good. I'm really cool with it all. I mean, whatever, right? Whatevah, ha, ha, ha, ha, ha, ha, ha!" The forced laugh was the spookiest part of her hysteria.

"Sophie." I tried to hug her.

"Don't touch me!" She squealed and ran from the room.

"She's fine," Alistair stated.

"Oh, yeah," I said. We both lit cigarettes with trembling hands. My phone rang. "Yeah?"

"Jilldo, come see me."

"Seriously, Chief? You've heard about the weather?"

"Not a word."

"Be right there." I stood up and started layering clothes. "Chief needs a kiss," I explained to Alistair. He held up the car keys.

I stumbled down the ice-clogged walk and frowned at the gray sky. The north wind sheared branches from the trees that landed with clattering explosions on the ice below. I felt ice grains start pecking my neck. I got in the car and drove with dread across town.

"So....how are you?" Chief St. John steepled his fingers over his steaming coffee. His home had power and his children were watching television too loudly in the family room.

"Fine," I said curtly. "Why the summons?" Oops—warning sign one. Chief kept tabs on the emotional health of the police department, homicide specifically and me in particular. He had an uncanny intuition for when to send detectives on vacation. He claimed it prevented burnout and kept detectives from the creeping compulsion to make the department their whole lives. It kept marriages and families together and sleeping bags and toothbrushes out of the office and the detectives closer to whole and balanced.

"Shutting down and clamming up. Not good, Jill."

"Aw, come on, I'm fine. I answered fine because I am fine so I said fine."

"Jilldo, remember your test scores?"

"Chief, that was more than a decade ago. What does that have to do with *anything?*"

"Are you listening?"

"With both ears."

"You're like an animal. You are barely literate, but goddamn, your instincts are good."

"Eat me."

"Mine are too. And you've been on watch."

"For what?" I said.

"Numbness of the heart."

"Oh, Jesus, Mary, and Joseph, would you grow a pair?"

"Denial and defensive, strike two."

"Fuck you! It's an icetastrophe! I've been cooped up and barely working as it is! You're a tool!"

"Rage, strike three. You're on vacation."

"Like hell. If I were, I wouldn't be here with you."

"Witty." Then over his shoulder, "Matilda! Turn that television down!" Then to me, "Jim called."

"Oh, so *that's* what this is about. Why didn't you say so?"

"He's a pain in my ass, so I'm passing that pain on to you."

"Trickle down leadership," I said. My phone rang. "Perryman? What you know good?"

"It worked!" Perryman said. "Goodson wrecked his car speeding on the ice, and Oklahoma County deputies picked him up outside Norman. He's in custody and they administered the polygraph and got a confession!"

I stood up, exhilarated. "He didn't invoke?" I was talking about his Miranda rights.

"Nope. I think he was just exhausted and ready to crack. When will the courthouse be open?"

"I don't know. They will arraign him by video. I'm sure both of us will need to testify in prelim. I doubt he will waive that," I said.

"See you in court!"

Chief St. John waited for me to explain. Just as I started to tell him, my phone rang. "Marny, what you know good?"

"A witness has contacted our office." Marny's voice was cautious and careful.

"About Goodson? He's already done."

"No…not Goodson."

I glanced at the chief. "Well?"

"It's Dewey Perryman's best friend."

I gasped. "Who is he? Is he there with you now?"

"His name is Ardell James. No, he's not here. We sent Honegger out to get a statement."

"Anything you can tell me now?"

"Just the sketchiest hints, but if this can be confirmed, this will blow up big."

I stomped my foot. "Like what?"

"Umm…Wanda and Dana were having an affair and Wanda threatened to expose it and Dana had her killed. Dana promised Ardell a lot of money and then never paid."

"Fuck!" My legs collapsed and I sat quickly. "Thanks, Marny." I hung up. "I'll explain later, Chief, but I've gotta go."

CHAPTER THIRTY-SEVEN

W here have you been?" Sophie demanded as I let myself into the house.

"Give it a rest. We're not married yet," I said, wrung out and exhausted from sparring with the chief and finding out about Perryman. Then tell her that instead of being a bionic blockhead, Marny lectured me. Fuck off, Marn.

Alistair sucked air, shook his newspaper, and raised it higher in front of his face. Sophie raised her eyebrows and looked like a cat sharpening her claws and preparing to pounce. "Oh, so I'm just your ice whore then, is that it?" she said, her voice scratchy and scarier than a scream.

I unwound my long muffler, took off my hat, gloves, and coat, and stood by the fire. "You don't pay a whore for sex," I barked, "You pay her to *leave.*"

"For God's sake, mate, make an effort!" Alistair said.

"Well, that's fascinating," Sophie said. "How do you get a rude, immature, self-centered mooch to leave? Dangle a pot of coffee outside?"

"Ouch!" I said sarcastically. "The first blow brings the blood, the second splatters it."

"I didn't know a douchebag had veins," Sophie said.

"I am in the violent crime biz, honey. I know blood."

Alistair slammed down the newspaper. "But does a douche have any bloody sense? All she asked was where you had been. Lighten up!"

Sophie and I glared at each other. "It's not what she asked, it's *how* she asked it," I said, feeling foolish.

"What a delicate flower," Sophie said sourly.

"I give up!" Alistair cried. "I'm going for a walk. I will be so happy when the airport opens, I will cry." He slammed the front door.

"So long, weasel," I said.

"What the fuck did he do?" Sophie said.

"Oh, nothing...I just...forget it." The fear and sadness were pushing up my throat to fill my mouth, but a great load of hate was on top, keeping me corked.

"Listen, you need to straighten up. I can't take this. I thought I could, but I can't. It's too hard. You're unstable and unpredictable and it's not exciting. I get pulled into your tornado when I'm just standing here, minding my own business and trying to care."

The hate in my gut got hotter and meaner. Marny cowered in a corner. "You're breaking up with me?" I stated, each syllable sharp as a shard of iced glass.

Sophie shrugged. "Look at it from my side. Look at the cost benefit analysis."

"Cost benefit analysis?" Each word was frost bitten.

"One—you're not really here. Only default here. Two—you seem ambivalent about me just like before." To her credit, it was Sophie's only reference to the last time we tried to make it years ago and I took off and broke her heart. "Three," she continued, "you're a psycho. I never know when you'll be horny, happy, hungry, mad, or sad. You should see someone. Even if you are a tough cop, it shouldn't be a roller coaster to that extreme."

"Who is he?" I said. That shocked her into silence. "Who is the motherfucker? I'll kick his ass! I'll throw him in jail!"

"See?" Sophie said. "This is exactly why right here! You didn't hear a word I said and immediately fabricated a reason I'm dumping your sorry ass. There is no *him*. It's not *me;* it's *you*."

"Well, we will see about that," I said. I flung open Alistair's laptop and pulled up a site for WSW singles. I perched an unlit cigarette on my lip and played with my Zippo.

"What the hell are you doing?" Sophie's voice was soft and incredulous with wonder.

"Moving on," I said. I put an unlit cigarette in my mouth and randomly chose a singles site and picked the menu to compose an ad. "Hot cop seeking sexy femme for LTR." I typed angrily, hitting the keyboard with unnecessary viciousness and recited, "Must be—" I looked Sophie up and down, who seemed shocked into speechless immobility, "voluptuous. Blonde." I pondered. "Brave and loyal." My spine was stiff and straight and righteous. "Generous. Forgiving."

Sophie touched me on the shoulder so tenderly, it unraveled my thoughts. "Dumb, stupid, foolish."

I had typed stupid before I realized what I was doing. "Must like non-stop drama more than a Greek chorus. Must enjoy sniveling and be batshit wingnut hyper-crazy." Sophie's voice was as sweet and soft as cotton candy. It drained all my poison. I tried to gather it back, but it darted away like drops of mercury.

"What else?" I asked wearily, my hands poised above the keys.

"Moody. Difficult. Demanding. Labor intensive. Workaholic." I closed my eyes and typed. "Oblivious, self-centered, abominably selfish, indecisive," Sophie continued, her words gaining speed, her voice gaining volume.

"Wait," I said.

"No, I'm just now stretched and warmed up." Sophie swung her arms and pulled on each of her wrists.

"Are you serious about all of these?" I pointed at the paragraph.

"Hell yes!" Sophie said. Then she rummaged in a bookshelf and brought out *Roget's Thesaurus*. She pulled up an ottoman and sat, popped her fingers and sighed happily. "All righty, let's begin again," Sophie said, shuffling the book's pages.

"No." I crossed my arms over my chest. Even my flattop felt extra-bristly and angry.

"Why are you so red?" Sophie was as bright and frisky as a newborn lamb.

"Fuck you!" I said, my lips still clamped around my cig.

"Defensive," Sophie pronounced, reaching around me to type the word with one finger.

I shuddered, surrendering. "Is all that true?"

"Yes, absolutely," Sophie said, studying the word *incorrigible* in *Roget's*.

I blinked. My eyes hurt. I felt pulled to the bottom of a hopeless lake. "Then I'll never find anyone." Sophie stopped after typing *bossy* and gazed at me.

"No, you're right." I felt gray with sadness. "I'm a complete shit and I'll always be alone and I'll hurt anyone who gets close. Type that!" Sophie stared at me. "Type it!" I thundered. She typed: *funny* and *passionate*.

We paused in silence for a few seconds, the energy draining and the mood shifting. "Who would love me?" I asked. I threw my dry cigarette to the floor. I rubbed my Zippo and replaced it in my pocket. I stared at the facts on the screen. "Who would love me?" I repeated faintly. I turned the chair toward Sophie whose face was an impassive mask. "Do you know anyone who could love someone like that?" I jerked my thumb at the computer.

She shook her head silently, her eyes large and dark and scared. I pulled the ottoman close between my legs. "Do you?" I whispered.

"Absolutely not," Sophie whispered back.

"I didn't think so." I nuzzled her hair.

With a gasp, Sophie burst out crying. "Stop. Don't. Have mercy on me, Jill. Have mercy. I can't." Tears flowed down her face in a stream, collected at her chin and dropped to the floor. Precious fluid, I thought incoherently.

"Okay, okay, okay..." I said, "I won't. Of course not. No. Sh, baby. Sh. Don't worry."

"Jill..." Sophie sobbed, "please understand."

"Sh, Sophie, I do. I do." I hugged her to me and felt rotten for creating the quakes she was going through as I held fast. When she calmed, I broke our embrace and handed her some tissues from the box on the desk. "Sophie…it's clear I need to change."

Sophie, wiping her nose, stared at me, her face washed clean. "I know about you."

"Oh, yeah? This ought to be good."

"You're not tough at all. This is a self-destructive façade."

"A what?"

"You avoid love because it's hard. Crime is clean. But let me tell you, it won't nourish your soul and give you the big O and hold you and bring you coffee."

"And you will?" I fondled my Zippo.

"Absolutely not. So really, what's your problem? Are you really a love-starved but terrified loner? Please tell me you're not that cliché."

"Well." I swallowed a lump of cotton lodged in my throat. "I've never talked about this before." I stared at my feet. Marny would want me to take this risk, I thought.

"Do you want to tell me?" Sophie asked with such a tone that all my locks unlatched.

"Yes." I felt sodden with anguish. "Yes."

Then I must've left my body for several minutes because Sophie prompted me by saying, "Do you want to tell me now or another time?"

I couldn't look at her. "Now," I whispered. "My job is…my job is *me*. It's not like being a mortgage banker, car salesman or…a hair stylist. I have no set schedule. I'm never off-duty, you get it? Let's say we get together and it's all good and then you start calling me and saying, 'When are you coming home?' And the answer always is and always will be, when the work is done. I can't promise you a goddamn thing. Whomever I'm with, she comes second. Always. I wouldn't treat a dog that way. That's why I've never gotten one." I clicked my Zippo until Sophie put her hand gently on mine. I still didn't look up. "You know, when someone has been drinking and he's killed, if there's blood spilled, you can smell the alcohol at the scene?"

"No, I didn't know that."

"To count how many times a vic was stabbed, count the cast-off spray streaks, and add one."

I heard Sophie suck in her breath. I knew I was rambling, but she had opened Pandora's murder book now. Too late to stop. "I can't sleep anymore. But if I do sleep, I see dead people in my dreams. There's nothing that can erase what I've seen and I can never forget."

Sophie moved closer to kneel at my feet, but she didn't try to meet my eyes.

"One of my first cases was a baby. A baby! He had roasted alive on a floor furnace because his little walker got stuck in the grate and his parents weren't around. When we found his parents, they were felony addicts. All of us in the department chipped in for a headstone." I saw movement and I sneaked a look at Sophie. She had covered her ears with both hands.

"One of my last cases with Kendall was an abducted woman kept locked twenty-four seven under a couple's waterbed. They got picked up for drug possession and she starved to death chained in that box. It was high summer and the meter reader smelled her body. She had melted into the wood floor." I choked. "The ME's office had to shovel her remains into a body bag. Crime scene clean up couldn't do much, it had soaked so deep. The city just tore down the house."

Sophie's shoulders were shaking.

"I'm afraid all the time. I don't remember what it's like not to be. Animals only kill for necessity. Humans kill because they want to. I never know what's behind the door, under the house, in the attic, in that car I'm chasing. If a cop tells you he isn't scared, run away, don't walk. Because he's either lying or crazy. And I can't let any of this affect my job. I've just gotta stuff it and keep moving.

Keep working. Because I'm bringing justice. I know that sounds corny, but when you tell a grieving family that you got him, there's nothing sweeter in life. When you're in court and you get that guilty verdict, there's nothing better. Nothing. And all this," I gestured around my head, "is something that not even the best love," I smiled tenderly, "can help or heal."

"But other detectives have spouses and families." Sophie wiped her eyes.

I shrugged. "I don't know what to tell you. They're better than I am."

Sophie caressed my boot, still staring at the floor. "I don't believe that."

"That's the fantasy that will get your heart broken."

"I've been heartbroken before and here I am, at your feet. Aren't some things, some *people* worth the risk?"

I sat in silence for a long time. Finally, I whispered, "That's why I'm telling you the truth." My Zip was uncharacteristically still. Sophie nodded. I caressed her hair.

"I think homicide cops are born, not made. It's a calling, like being a doctor or a teacher. If you're meant to be one, it will find you, regardless of where you are."

"Not like a mortgage banker?" Sophie laughed dryly.

"Right. Murder happens because people allow emotions to cloud their judgment and logic. What is love but emotion? I can't do that."

"Not even for me?"

"No." I sighed shakily, clutching my Zippo. Hard, clean, well-defined metal edges and easy machinery. "I should've been a fireman. Everyone hates a cop, but loves a fireman."

Sophie snorted and dared a glance at me. "That's not why you do this."

I closed my eyes. I felt Sophie embrace me. She put her lips against my ear. "Please trust me. I can handle it. But I can't prove that to you unless you let me. Please."

I pushed her away. My eyes felt swollen, my heart hollow. But Sophie with her tear-stained face and red nose, looked luminous.

We stared at each other until I cleared the clog in my throat. "I would never ask you otherwise, but..." I shocked myself at what I was about to say. "Would you consider....baby steps?" I blurted before I could stop myself.

"Baby steps?" Sophie sniffled, blowing her nose.

"Baby steps." I took her hand as gently as if it were an injured and skittish wild animal's paw. "Just one tiny step. And then if that's okay, one more. But nothing big, nothing fast, nothing guaranteed."

"Baby steps?" Sophie repeated, her voice blooming.

"Baby steps."

"Let me think about it," Sophie said and surprised me by blushing.

"Yes, yes, you think. Take all the time you want. Whatever you need is all right. Just think and we'll talk again. I'll change; I promise," I babbled euphorically.

My phone rang. Perryman.

CHAPTER THIRTY-EIGHT

Perryman wanted me to meet her at her house, but I wasn't sure where she was. I heard gunshots. Could be hunters or Perryman. I parked half a mile away and approached through the woods. My hands were frigid and quickly losing feeling and dexterity. I passed the burn pit and took photos of it. Jonathan ran by, his bell jingling merrily. He ran halfway up a pine tree, jumped down, and rubbed against my legs. He obviously loved snow and ice. I caressed him while watching the house. My finger accidentally caught on his collar. The pet cam! My hands were rapidly going numb from the bitter cold, but I checked Jonathan's collar and it snapped open easily. I tucked the collar with the attached camera into my parka pocket, and the bell tinkled a final time as I patted it inside my coat. Jonathan, seemingly happy and surprised to be collar-free, took off, his bright orange tail straight up and his muscular body zooming joyfully toward a pin oak.

"Rogers?" Perryman called from a distance. I saw her approaching me. When she finally got within ten yards, she smirked and said, "You know, don't you? Here we are, the coup de grace."

"I don't speak Spanish. Just plain talk is all I need."

"You're dead."

"Perryman, I don't know what you're talking about. I came because you called." I played goofy and stupid. "Sure is a sweet cat you have." I gestured behind me at the trees. "He likes the weather, huh? So what you know good? More news about Rick?"

"Nope," Perryman said. I saw her gun was dangling loosely from her right hand.

"Relax, Dana. I'm not sure why I'm here. Just be cool. Everything is fine."

"Ardell?" Perryman said.

"I don't know who that is. Another cat?"

"I cannot believe that anyone would trust him over me! You know he's an ex con. And when an ex con waives his rights, you *know* he's going to lie his ass off. His second page has to be measured in pounds, not pages!"

"Calm down. If you want to explain what you're talking about, start at the beginning," I said.

"Ardell wanted to fuck me! He tried to rape me and I told him I was going to file charges on him, so anything he says is just revenge."

"Just tell me everything from the start. I'm not going to hurt you. I didn't even bring my gun." A bluff, but I didn't want to shoot her.

"Stupid decision." She raised her pistol, and in that split second, I dove for a snow bank. The bullet grazed my calf. From being riddled with past bullet scars, I knew it would take a while to start hurting, so I cowered in the snow drift realizing that almost no bulletproof vests were made of snow. I crab-crawled to a thicket of trees.

"Sheriff, you need to turn yourself in! I cannot guarantee your safety!" I fumbled for my gun, but my hands were completely numb and I couldn't get it out of the holster.

Perryman laughed. "Always the superior cop, even on your knees."

"Jim's office is issuing a warrant for you right now. He's scheduling a press conference. Make it easy on yourself." It was another bluff, of course. But that was a big part of law enforcement.

"Did they tell you I'm the fall guy? The DA Jim and his pal, my nasty ass predecessor, Sheriff Stanley, were best buddies from way back when Jesus was a boy."

I didn't believe this conspiracy fantasy for a second, but I also knew the corruption of the DA's office, so anything was possible. "Yes, I know. But if you hadn't killed Wanda, they wouldn't have anything on you!"

Perryman replied by sending another bullet singing by my head. She wasn't sure exactly where I was so that spoiled her accuracy. My hand twitched for wanting my Zippo or my gun. I kept trying to warm my hands enough to get a grip on my Glock, but my fingers were like blocks of wood.

"They want to appoint some pet of theirs to have a stranglehold of control on the entire county!"

"Yeah, the world is wrong. It's unjust and unfair, and *fuck God in the eyeball!*" I shouted. "But why kill me?"

Perryman punctuated her answer with shots. "Because." Shot. "You." Shot. "Deserve." Shot. "It." Shot.

I didn't want to die, but I couldn't disagree with her. As a cop, I liked deciding and dispensing justice, and Perryman did too. She had tried and convicted me. She would never be able to trap Jesus Jim or Sheriff Stanley in the woods for a manhunt, so here I was, the next best thing. The most dangerous, and exciting, game.

"Come out, you coward!" Perryman yelled. "We can just talk."

"Like you talked Wanda into her grave?" I shouted. I regretted saying that. There was no point. I would be better served by my own silence. Bullets tore through the trees. I fumbled with my radio and even with wooden fingers, was able to press the button and I requested SWAT.

"I can hear you, dummy. They can't help you because I'm loaded for bear. You'll be a red spot in the snow before they can even gear up." I heard Perryman's boots crunching, looking for me. "Come on out, tough guy. Face me!"

Face her? I had already peed my britches a little. When I had been hit with gunshot in the past, it was accidental, collateral damage. I had never been specifically hunted.

When she got close enough to see my trail of blood, I knew I couldn't outrun her, so I dropped to my knees and leaned my head back. "Here I am, Perryman." My legs were shaking and my hands trembling. I thought of Sophie. My car. My home. My job. All the meals I would never eat, all the drinks I wouldn't drink, all the laughter I would miss, the sunsets, the seasons, the holidays. I had never been to Hawaii. Death scenes are never grand enough. These ordinary woods with brush piles and birds singing in the branches would be my last vision on earth. Shouldn't it be finer than this? More momentous? Tears sprang to my eyes and oozed down my face.

"Come on, Perryman," I choked out in a hoarse whisper. "What do you have to gain by killing me?" My leg was beginning to throb.

"The question is: what do I have to lose? Nothing. And you've been begging for this for years, haven't you?" Perryman approached and cocked the Glock.

I nodded, my face wet, my chin trembling, my eyes closed.

"Well, here it comes at last," Perryman said. The gun dry clicked. "Fuck!"

I opened my eyes. Perryman needed to reload. I lunged for her weapon and felt the blow like an explosion as she hit me in the face with the pistol, knocking me on my ass in the snow. The surprise and shock of not being killed was so great, I huddled on all fours and vomited.

"Look at you. You're pathetic," Perryman said and turned to finish reloading.

In two seconds, I spat, scooped snow over my mess, put a handful of clean snow into my mouth, and stood. Perryman's back was to me, and so I launched myself into the air and tackled her—wresting the Glock from her loosened grip first thing. My hands were awkward, but I was able to keep the gun in a clumsy hold. I had knocked the wind out of her so I held Perryman down with my knee in her back as I put her gun in my waistband and took ten times as long as I should have to zip-tie her wrists together. But I had a hundred pounds on Perryman and she couldn't move.

"Should've finished the job," I said into her ear. "You never," I grunted as I lifted her to her knees, "turn your back," I jerked her, stumbling, to her feet, "on your enemy."

"You're making a terrible mistake!" Perryman said. "You don't know anything! Let me go this instant and I'll do all I can to help you."

"And this," I fished an old bandana out of my coat pocket, balled it up, and stuffed it in her mouth, "is for your own safety." I pulled her, walking toward the car. "Because you haven't been Mirandized, and if I have to listen to one more second of your blah blah, I'll kill you."

We walked without speaking the half mile through the ice and trees to Sophie's car.

I drove slowly through the ice toward the jail, Perryman a stoic, bound and gagged statue next to me. The flesh wound on my leg throbbed, but due to the cold, it had clotted.

"What about this weather?" I asked with a grin.

Perryman blew out the gag with a grunt, and it lay in a wet wad in her lap. "I'll die before I let you take me to jail."

I braked for dramatic effect, but the car fishtailed and swerved into the curb. The car behind us honked long and hard, clipping the taillight of Sophie's car as it passed, the driver flipping me off. "You satisfied that's what you want?" I said, my eyes narrowed. Perryman tugged the cuffs binding her wrists behind her. Then she faced forward without answering.

When we arrived at the jail, Perryman wouldn't go inside. I ensured she was totally secure with no chance of escape, and I went to the booking desk to request assistance. I could see Sophie's car from the desk, so I kept watch on it.

"You look like fuck pie," Deputy Cooter said.

"I'll have a slice of that," said Britney, the booking officer.

"A la mode?" I said.

"Natch."

"All this is makin' me hungry." Cooter rubbed his belly. "I'm having to eat my wife's cookin' because ain't nothing open. I'd kill for a fried onion burger."

"I need someone to help me bring in a defendant. And I need a cell in protective custody, not with the general population."

"Well, we're on skeleton staff right now," Britney said.

I put my hands on the counter, leaned to within three inches of her face, and repeated, "*I need all available badges and an isolated cell.*"

Britney paled and ran off in search of help. Deputy Cooter smiled, putting a toothpick in the space of his missing front teeth, and pointed outside. "Who you got out there? Timothy McVeigh is dead." Then he guffawed.

I just stared at him.

CHAPTER THIRTY-NINE

In her cell, Perryman grinned like a shark at me. "I never thought I would say this, but thank God for this weather, otherwise, my....*temporary* incarceration...would be a media circus. And Jim isn't ready with his press conference and not much press around to film it. Lucky break, eh?"

I clicked my Zippo and watched her without blinking.

Perryman continued, "You know...I had heard of you before my promotion. I studied your methods. I was convinced I wouldn't be caught." She spat on the floor near my boots. My mind raced incoherently to the misdemeanor charge of "Placing Bodily Fluids on Law Enforcement Officer."

"You broke my heart," I told her, and then, shocked by the squirt of water to my eyes, I stared at the ceiling.

"Fuck off," Perryman said, flopping on her bunk with a sigh. "I've got bigger worries now." She rolled to face the wall.

After leaving the jail, I called the homicide division to see if there were any working computers. Only one, I was told, but I could get in line. When I got there, I pulled rank to view the photos on the pet cam. There were 500 shots on the memory card. As I scrolled through whopper-jawed images of birds, pictures of whiskers looking out from under vehicles, views of neighborhood crawl spaces, shots from high up in trees and a near-capture of a squirrel, I saw evidence of Perryman murdering Wanda. I couldn't believe it!

My heart began pounding and my breath came quickly. That crazy cat Jonathan had caught the murder on his digital camera! It had happened outside, about an hour before sunset, so the light was good, and Jonathan must have been very interested in whatever was happening because he stayed put long enough for the camera to get the entire crime. A shooting only takes a second, so Jonathan just as easily could've run by and missed the entire thing. But after studying the images more closely, I saw what had kept the cat interested. There was a possum hiding in a tree hollow a few yards from Perryman's feet. The possum's eyes fluoresced in the photos.

The dismemberment was not on the pet cam, and I was grateful for that. Thank God for curious cats. I printed the crime scene photos, bagged and labeled it all, and turned it in to forensics. This was another first.

After leaving the office, I drove slowly to the cemetery, something I did when I needed to feel close to Kendall. I was surprised to see the gates open and the drive clear and sanded. There were many cars already there. I supposed the weather brought out the sorrow and thoughts of mortality in a lot of us. I parked and walked carefully to Kendall's burial plot. I passed a family putting toys on a child's grave, an old man chipping ice off of a tombstone and a woman struggling with a child's sand shovel and pail to unsuccessfully clear the ground around a monument.

At Kendall's gravestone, I saw that someone had been there before me and had left a bouquet of roses. I walked around the monument and saw someone had spray-painted "sueeee" on the marble. I was instantly enraged, but like almost everything else, cleaning off the graffiti would have to wait until warmer temperatures. I took off my parka and draped it over the tombstone to cover the word painted in lurid red.

"How are you, Papa?" I said, then checked to make sure I wasn't overheard. The cemetery was pristine. Not a single branch, twig, or tree out of place. Anger at the tombstone defacing kept me warm without my coat. "I don't know how I'm doing." I paced in a tight circuit as I spoke. "You know about all this mess?" I gestured to the threatening gray sky. "All this ice. Christ. The hospitals and nursing homes were in real danger for a while. The jail was too, but we don't care about that, do we?" My laugh was a bark. "But other states delivered a shit ton of giant emergency generators, so no one died from loss of power. Just from murder." I snorted another small laugh. "So that's how the town is. I think I'm getting better. I believe I may actually be recovering after...after you...I mean...after you *died.*" I was able to say the word aloud, which was an improvement. "I just wish you hadn't. Don't you know I still need you?" As soon as I said it, I was overwhelmed by the feeling that I didn't. I was okay on my own and that I was ready. Kendall left me in charge and I could do it. My knees gave out, and I sat in front of Papa's stone, indifferent to the ice. "Well, I'll miss you forever, you sumbitch." I crossed my legs and sat smoking until the falling ice forced me to leave. I left my parka on the tombstone.

Epilogue

One bright morning, twenty-seven days after the initial ice storm, the sun emerged and stayed. People who had fled the state for the holidays returned home. The temps soared to the mid-thirties, and the ice melted like heavy spring rain. The gutters ran deep with icy rivers; the streets steamed with evaporation; the waterlogged dirt turned to soggy mud; people carried umbrellas in the sunshine to protect themselves from the melting downpour.

The airport opened at last, and Sophie and I chauffeured Alistair to his flight.

The ice moved east; turning to thunderstorms over the mid-southern states; the meteorologists gleefully predicted temperatures above freezing for the next two weeks.

Tulsa was stranded, a disaster area, sopping, soaking wet, and still mostly powerless. About a million and a half people were still without electricity. The interstate power crews remained on three round-the-clock shifts. The massive cleanup of the arboreal holocaust began. Chainsaws ran day and night from every direction. City parks were used as impromptu green dumps, and mountains of discarded wood grew. The tons of dead trees became so massive, they began to attract tourists. Insurance companies worked around the clock. Every person in Tulsa had at least one claim for damage. I packed a bag and unpacked it at Sophie's, using one slim, shallow, hard-won drawer. Jesus Jim was caught in a sting of his own involving sex with men in the bathrooms of the courthouse. A new sheriff was appointed, and I made no effort to meet him.

My new phone rang. "Rogers!" I barked, clicking my Zippo and enjoying a smoke on Sophie's shining, soaked patio. My coffee mug sent delicious curls of heat into the dripping air. Tree limbs crashed around me.

"A murder," Chief said, "Little Mexico. Head over there now."

"Yes, sir. On my way."

The End

About the Author

Clara Nipper is a writer, and when not writing, she makes desserts and enlarges her certified wildlife habitat garden which is home to both humane beehives and happy hens. Clara installed a Little Free Library to serve the community with free books anytime. Clara also skates for Roughneck Roller Derby under the derby name Cat Owta Hell, and she sculls with Tulsa Rowing Club. Additionally, she has established Sounds Good Studios for which she is both narrator and producer. Like writing, Clara loves the work because she loves words and stories. www.claranipper.org

Books Available from Bold Strokes Books

A Reunion to Remember by TJ Thomas. Reunited after a decade, Jo Adams and Rhonda Black must navigate a significant age difference, family dynamics, and their own desires and fears to explore an opportunity for love. (978-1-62639-534-3)

Built to Last by Aurora Rey. When Professor Olivia Bennett hires contractor Joss Bauer to restore her dilapidated farmhouse, she learns her heart, as much as her house, is in need of a renovation. (978-1-62639-552-7)

Capsized by Julie Cannon. What happens when a woman turns your life completely upside down? (978-1-62639-479-7)

Girls With Guns by Ali Vali, Carsen Taite, and Michelle Grubb. Three stories by three talented crime writers—Carsen Taite, Ali Vali, and Michelle Grubb—each packing her own special brand of heat. (978-1-62639-585-5)

Heartscapes by MJ Williamz. Will Odette ever recover her memory or is Jesse condemned to remember their love alone? (978-1-62639-532-9)

Murder on the Rocks by Clara Nipper. Detective Jill Rogers lives with two things on her mind: sex and murder. While an ice storm cripples Tulsa, two things stand in Jill's way: her lover and the DA. (978-1-62639-600-5)

Necromantia by Sheri Lewis Wohl. When seeing dead people is more than a movie tagline. (978-1-62639-611-1)

Salvation by I. Beacham. Claire's long-term partner now hates her, for all the wrong reasons, and she sees no future until she meets

Regan, who challenges her to face the truth and find love. (978-1-62639-548-0)

Trigger by Jessica Webb. Dr. Kate Morrison races to discover how to defuse human bombs while learning to trust her increasingly strong feelings for the lead investigator, Sergeant Andy Wyles. (978-1-62639-669-2)

24/7 by Yolanda Wallace. When the trip of a lifetime becomes a pitched battle between life and death, will anyone survive? (978-1-62639-6-197)

A Return to Arms by Sheree Greer. When a police shooting makes national headlines, activists Folami and Toya struggle to balance their relationship and political allegiances, a struggle intensified after a fiery young artist enters their lives. (978-1-62639-6-814)

After the Fire by Emily Smith. Paramedic Connor Haus is convinced her time for love has come and gone, but when firefighter Logan Curtis comes into town, she learns it may not be too late after all. (978-1-62639-6-524)

Dian's Ghost by Justine Saracen. The road to genocide is paved with good intentions. (978-1-62639-5-947)

Fortunate Sum by M. Ullrich. Financial advisor Catherine Carter lives a calculated life, but after a collision with spunky Imogene Harris (her latest client) and unsolicited predictions, Catherine finds herself facing an unexpected variable: Love. (978-1-62639-5-305)

Soul to Keep by Rebekah Weatherspoon. What *won't* a vampire do for love… (978-1-62639-6-166)

When I Knew You by KE Payne. Eight letters, three friends, two lovers, one secret. Can the past ever be forgiven? (978-1-62639-5-626)

Wild Shores by Radclyffe. Can two women on opposite sides of an oil spill find a way to save both a wildlife sanctuary and their hearts? (978-1-62639-6-456)

Love on Tap by Karis Walsh. Beer and romance are brewing for Tace Lomond when archaeologist Berit Katsaros comes into her life. (987-1-162639-564-0)

Love on the Red Rocks by Lisa Moreau. An unexpected romance at a lesbian resort forces Malley to face her greatest fears where she must choose between playing it safe or taking a chance at true happiness. (987-1-162639-660-9)

Tracker and the Spy by D. Jackson Leigh. There are lessons for all when Captain Tanisha is assigned untried pyro Kyle and a lovesick dragon horse for a mission to track the leader of a dangerous cult. (987-1-162639-448-3)

Whirlwind Romance by Kris Bryant. Will chasing the girl break Tristan's heart or give her something she's never had before? (987-1-162639-581-7)

Whiskey Sunrise by Missouri Vaun. Culture and religion collide when Lovey Porter, daughter of a local Baptist minister, falls for the handsome thrill-seeking moonshine runner, Royal Duval. (987-1-162639-519-0)

Dyre: By Moon's Light by Rachel E. Bailey. A young werewolf, Des, guards the aging leader of all the Packs: the Dyre. Stable employment—nice work, if you can get it...at least until silver bullets start to fly. (978-1-62639-6-623)

Fragile Wings by Rebecca S. Buck. In Roaring Twenties London, can Evelyn Hopkins find love with Jos Singleton or will the scars of the Great War crush her dreams? (978-1-62639-5-466)

Live and Love Again by Jan Gayle. Jessica Whitney could be Sarah Jarret's second chance at love, but their differences and Sarah's grief continue to come between their budding relationship. (978-1-62639-5-176)

Starstruck by Lesley Davis. Actress Cassidy Hayes and writer Aiden Darrow find out the hard way not all life-threatening drama is confined to the TV screen or the pages of a manuscript. (978-1-62639-5-237)

Stealing Sunshine by Tina Michele. Under the Central Florida sun, two women struggle between fear and love as a dangerous plot of deception and revenge threatens to steal priceless art and lives. (978-1-62639-4-452)

The Fifth Gospel by Michelle Grubb. Hiding a Vatican secret is dangerous—sharing the secret suicidal—can Felicity survive a perilous book tour, and will her PR specialist, Anna, be there when it's all over? (978-1-62639-4-476)

Cold to the Touch by Cari Hunter. A drug addict's murder is the start of a dangerous investigation for Detective Sanne Jensen and Dr. Meg Fielding, as they try to stop a killer with no conscience. (978-1-62639-526-8)

Forsaken by Laydin Michaels. The hunt for a killer teaches one woman that she must overcome her fear in order to love, and another that success is meaningless without happiness. (978-1-62639-481-0)

Infiltration by Jackie D. When a CIA breach is imminent, a Marine instructor must stop the attack while protecting her heart from being disarmed by a recruit. (978-1-62639-521-3)

Midnight at the Orpheus by Alyssa Linn Palmer. Two women desperate to make their way in the world, a man hell-bent on revenge, and a cop risking his career: all in a day's work in Capone's Chicago. (978-1-62639-607-4)

Spirit of the Dance by Mardi Alexander. Major Sorla Reardon's return to her family farm to heal threatens Riley Johnson's safe life when small-town secrets are revealed, and love may not conquer all. (978-1-62639-583-1)

Sweet Hearts by Melissa Brayden, Rachel Spangler, and Karis Walsh. Do you ever wonder *Whatever happened to…*? Find out when you reconnect with your favorite characters from Melissa Brayden's *Heart Block*, Rachel Spangler's *LoveLife*, and Karis Walsh's *Worth the Risk*. (978-1-62639-475-9)

Totally Worth It by Maggie Cummings. Who knew there's an all-lesbian condo community in the NYC suburbs? Join twentysomething BFFs Meg and Lexi at Bay West as they navigate friendships, love, and everything in between. (978-1-62639-512-1)

Illicit Artifacts by Stevie Mikayne. Her foster mother's death cracked open a secret world Jil never wanted to see…and now she has to pick up the stolen pieces. (978-1-62639-472-8)

Pathfinder by Gun Brooke. Heading for their new homeworld, Exodus's chief engineer Adina Vantressa and nurse Briar Lindemay carry game-changing secrets that may well cause them to lose everything when disaster strikes. (978-1-62639-444-5)

Prescription for Love by Radclyffe. Dr. Flannery Rivers finds herself attracted to the new ER chief, city girl Abigail Remy, and the incendiary mix of city and country, fire and ice, tradition and change is combustible. (978-1-62639-570-1)

Ready or Not by Melissa Brayden. Uptight Mallory Spencer finds relinquishing control to bartender Hope Sanders too tall an order in fast-paced New York City. (978-1-62639-443-8)

Summer Passion by MJ Williamz. Women loving women is forbidden in 1946 Hollywood, yet Jean and Maggie strive to keep their love alive and away from prying eyes. (978-1-62639-540-4)

The Princess and the Prix by Nell Stark. "Ugly duckling" Princess Alix of Monaco was resigned to loneliness until she met racecar driver Thalia d'Angelis. (978-1-62639-474-2)

Winter's Harbor by Aurora Rey. Lia Brooks isn't looking for love in Provincetown, but when she discovers chocolate croissants and pastry chef Alex McKinnon, her winter retreat quickly starts heating up. (978-1-62639-498-8)

The Time Before Now by Missouri Vaun. Vivian flees a disastrous affair, embarking on an epic, transformative journey to escape her past, until destiny introduces her to Ida, who helps her rediscover trust, love, and hope. (978-1-62639-446-9)